Also by Elissa Janine Hoole

Sometimes Never, Sometimes Always
Kiss the Morning Star

THE
MEMORY
JAR

THE
MEMORY
JAR

Elissa Janine Hoole

Woodbury, Minnesota

First Edition
Second Printing, 2016

Book design by Bob Gaul
Cover design by Lisa Novak
Cover image by getty/175816888/©sah

Flux, an imprint of Llewellyn Worldwide Ltd.

Library of Congress Cataloging-in-Publication Data
Names: Hoole, Elissa Janine, author.
Title: The memory jar / Elissa Janine Hoole.
Description: First edition. | Woodbury, Minnesota : Flux, [2016] |
    Summary: "Waiting for her boyfriend, Scott, to awaken from a coma after
    their snowmobile accident, seventeen-year-old Taylor isn't sure what
    Scott will remember from the night of the crash—or what she wants him
    to remember"—Provided by publisher.
Identifiers: LCCN 2015045468 (print) | LCCN 2016002605 (ebook) |
    ISBN 9780738747316 | ISBN 9780738748870 ()
Subjects: | CYAC: Memory—Fiction. | Coma—Fiction. | Secrets—Fiction.
Classification: LCC PZ7.H7667 Me 2016 (print) | LCC PZ7.H7667
    (ebook) | DDC [Fic]—dc23
LC record available at http://lccn.loc.gov/2015045468

Flux
Llewellyn Worldwide Ltd.
2143 Wooddale Drive
Woodbury, MN 55125-2989
www.fluxnow.com

Printed in the United States of America

To Creative Writing Club and the magic cards—
thanks to Maja, Symeon, Cecilia, Lillian,
Aspen, Ally, Evie, Rebekah, and Clayton.

NOW

Nobody blames me for what happened. They murmur these words like a lullaby chorus, their fingers gripping my shoulders, their breath in my hair. Scott's parents, his sister, our friends. Even the service dog in the waiting room gives me those sad eyes when I walk past and thumps his tail, twice, telling me it's okay. Nobody blames me.

But they should.

"You can't keep it," says Joey, glaring at me over the body of his brother draped in plastic tubing and medical tape. "You know that, right?"

I fold my hands into fists and wonder. Which secret does he know?

"It's not your decision," I say, and it doesn't matter. I'd give the same answer for both.

THEN

I was late. I didn't tell him because, hello? That shit is embarrassing. And besides, it was probably nothing. Stress, weight loss, whatever. And what was I going to tell him—what is there to say until you know? The test said you could find out with like 98 percent accuracy when you're only three days late, and I was five days, so I knocked the box off the drugstore shelf into my gigantic shoulder bag and then, you know. I peed on a stick.

It said three minutes. Three minutes is a long time, an eternity. My stomach hovered like a half inch above its normal position, the queasiness riding the buzz of my nerves. My phone counted down the seconds and then spit out this little chirp that made me jump, even though I was watching the numbers. What if everything changed? What if this was that one stupid thing, the one that screwed up my life? It would be a relief, maybe, to find out which of the world's evils would get me at last. My mom would be pleased to find out it wasn't meth or Internet creepers but ordinary sex that got me.

Not that the sex was ordinary. I mean, not that I had a lot to compare, god. Don't judge me. The overhead light in the public bathroom hummed for three minutes, and then I poked the plastic stick out from under the chunk of toilet paper I'd stuck on top of it to keep me from peeking and saw two thick lines in the pee stick, vivid. Pregnant. Vividly pregnant. My stomach lurched down from its perch, and I clapped my hand over my mouth.

NOW

I won't leave his room, but I hide in the little bathroom that marks Scott's progress from a bed in the ICU to an actual hospital room. I sit on the flimsy plastic lid of the toilet for twenty minutes at a stretch. I stare in the mirror and remember to breathe and type things that barely make sense into my phone. The psychologist I talked to after the regular doctors were done with me suggested that I "start the healing process" by writing down whatever comes to my mind, but all I can write about is Scott and the crash. I tell myself that if I can get it down, put it into words, I can make sense of this.

I finally muster the courage to go back out there, sit beside his bed and look at his face, but I can't stop thinking, *I was about to break up with you.* His chest moves with a rhythm so regular—like he's never had an emotion. What if he's different? What if he doesn't wake up? My hands burrow into the pocket of my hoodie.

Scott's sister brings me ginger ale, in a cup with ice. She brings me soda crackers as if she knows. Does she know? Joey glares and glares, and I twist my hands in my pocket, staring at Scott. Wondering about his head. The crunch of the impact still sticks like a song on repeat, and then the thought, again, *I was about to break up with you.*

"…come with?"

I blink, turning to look at Scott's sister, Emily, who stands in the doorway. I have no idea what she just said.

"Come on, Taylor." She reaches out to me like she's a mom and I'm a little kid, and I find myself reaching for her, too, and she squeezes my hand. My fingers squish together and I think about the ring, snug against my belly in the pocket of my sweatshirt, hidden from sight. Nobody knows, except maybe Joey, I don't know. Joey's a loose end.

Joey's staying put, crouched on the footstool, refusing to abandon his post.

"I can't," I say, but I let Emily pull me, even though I don't want Joey to win. It occurs to me that he might want to talk to his brother in private. But shouldn't it occur to him that I might want to talk to my boyfriend in private? To my ex-boyfriend? To my fiancé? I can't decide whether the ring should be on my finger when he wakes up or not. If he wakes up. Will he remember? If he doesn't, will I tell him?

"Order anything you want, sweetheart, except you have to get the decaf." Emily squeezes my hand again, and she must know, with a comment like that. She must. Did Scott tell his whole freaking family or what?

"You need to get some sleep," she says. "It's been hours and hours."

Sleep! Of course, she's talking about sleep. I exhale my relief and follow her out the door, to an elevator that drops three floors and makes my head spin so that I have to clutch the metal bar, and then I think about all the sick people who have clutched that bar and I feel kind of vulnerable. I don't know if I've ever felt like this before. I even follow Emily's directions and order a decaf.

There's a beat, a moment of actual silence. Emily and I pick at our raspberry scones and sip our coffee and breathe. For the first time in eighteen hours, I can nearly escape the constant refrain in my head. *I was about to break up with you.*

"They're going to start taking him off the coma medication," says Emily, still staring at her plate. "The swelling has slowed down." She looks up for a second, and our eyes collide. "He's going to be okay," she says.

I nod, but I can't swallow my food, and even though I know it's ridiculous, I swear I can feel my stomach swell out until it fills my sweatshirt, until the ring in the pocket is clearly outlined in the fabric and everyone can plainly see both of my secrets. What do I do with this knowledge—that my first slip of thought when she said that he would be okay was the hope that he wouldn't? No. Not a thought, even, not that solid. It's not even a feeling. It's a reflex, like when the doctor whacks that little rubber mallet against the soft spot beneath your knee cap. A jerk of a response, the instant I wanted Scott to die. *No*, god. Not to die. To forget, maybe.

"That's awesome," I manage to croak out. "That's amazing." It really is. We hit the snow ridge so hard—they say we both flew over the top, but I was lucky and landed in a snow drift. Scott hit the ice headfirst. The snow was packed into my ears, but I heard a crunch.

I lurch toward the restroom, abandoning Emily at the table.

THEN

I tossed it in the trash. It's not like it was the first time I'd ever thought about having Scott's baby. I mean, we've been together since I was fifteen and he was seventeen, which was, like, prime time in terms of daydreaming about the perfect future with my perfect husband in our perfect mansion (according to the game of chance Dani and I played in our notebooks), with our four children of above-average intelligence (according to the lines on my palm and the cryptic answers of Dani's Magic 8-Ball).

Exiting that bathroom, squinting my eyes a little against the glare of the lights and the scrubby people tugging their kids around by the arms, I didn't really feel any different. It was real, but it wasn't, and I didn't know what direction to walk so that people would stop noticing me. "There she goes, that pregnant girl," I was sure they were saying. "She was going to be a writer, or maybe a doctor, but now ... " There was so much to regret.

"She got knocked up in the passenger seat of her boyfriend's truck," said the next guy, glancing over from a display of cheap watches.

His wife followed his gaze, her eyes sliding over mine. "And do you know what she was thinking about when it happened?" she said, in my head.

"Whether her ACT scores were going to be in the mail," answered her husband, and both of them shook their heads sadly. Such a tragedy.

I shook my own head. *Jesus, Taylor. Get a grip.* Wish for a happy ending.

NOW

This is not a story like that, not a clever story about the girl who gets the boy and they share a magical kiss and become high school sweethearts and go off to college together and live long, happy lives. This isn't a story about a boy and a girl who have an accidental pregnancy and make the best of this wonderful gift by raising their child and fighting cancer and witnessing miracles and writing a best-selling memoir or something.

In this story, the girl is a monster and the boy is brain dead. Well, not exactly brain dead. Maybe that would be better, actually, you know? More picturesque and tragic, like a sad poem or a love story for women to weep over. Instead I have Scott, who lies here in some strange middle between alive and dead, and I have Joey, his eyes filled with hurt.

I have Understanding Emily, who maybe doesn't know. I have a little bathroom hideaway. I have an engagement ring and a break-up song. I have an empty space in my memory, followed by a crunch. I have one ugly laceration that starts at the peak of my forehead and slices its rude path down the bridge of my nose, across my bottom lip and ends on my chin, where I have one neat black stitch, hidden by a small bandage. And I have this creature swimming around in its little prison—a tiny cellular bundle right beneath my heart, which pumps it full of adrenaline and confusion and regret.

They paralyze you so you don't fight the ventilator. They've had him all doped up, in a medical coma. He hasn't been conscious at all except for that one second, his eyes opening wide and his mouth, like he was going to speak, and then nothing. I'm lulled by the sound of the machines, and Scott's mom clears her throat because she'd like us to leave.

"Just for a bit, let me sit with him," she says. They're bringing him back, fishing him out of that murky deep, or at least they're going to try. She pushes his hair back on his forehead like he's a little boy, but the bruising is darker now and it's hard to look. The surgeons shaved a patch on the side of his head in case they had to remove part of his skull. They haven't had to, which is, as Emily says, "a very good sign." If his brain stops swelling, recovery is more likely.

And I want Scott to get better, *obviously*, but there's a part of me—a miniscule part, I swear—that wanted to see what was inside his head. I can hear myself, whenever he would get too quiet, asking that stupid question: *What are you thinking?* Let me in, damn it.

I'm sleep-deprived, don't listen to me. I'm in shock. I'm pregnant. Whatever.

THEN

It wasn't easy, having my boyfriend leave for college. Oh *poor me*, I know, I'll roll my eyes along with you. And no, I wasn't messing around on him. I think that's what he thought, at first. "We were careful," he said. Yeah, no shit. Scott was *always* careful. He was the kind of guy who wore safety glasses to open the microwave and still worried. In fact, it's one of the things I remember most about Joey—the way he was always teasing Scott about being cautious, always thinking about consequences. Joey was the impulsive one, the reckless one. The one who ended up in some kind of treatment program for hurting himself or whatever. Joey should have been the one to end up with a pregnant girlfriend or a head injury.

Yeah, we were careful. Condoms, kid, that's what that means, because when you live in little Sterling Creek, Minnesota, so far north that even people from Duluth think you're in Canada, when your mom works in an office down the hall from the only Planned Parenthood in town and makes jokes about watching the "slutty girls" carrying their pee from the restroom, you don't necessarily get on birth control. Not unless you're into having uncomfortable discussions about what you're doing in your boyfriend's truck, which would be a disastrous conversation to have with my mother at least eighty-five percent of the time.

We established how careful we had been. "I mean, *really careful*, Taylor," he said, frowning. "Like I pulled out, even with the condom."

"I know, Scott. I know." Like he had the condom on before he left his house, basically. I should have kept the test, I guess, as proof or something, because apparently Scott was going to require some additional convincing that his child-thing was implanted in the wall of my uterus, right that very instant leeching the nutrients out of my bones. Secreting hormones that were making me feel half-crazy and one hundred percent queasy. "But you know. Still."

He didn't freak out. This isn't a sad story about an irresponsible boy who ran away from his knocked-up girlfriend, leaving her to turn to prostitution and smuggling drugs across the border (of Minnesota?) in her dirty infant carrier. It also isn't a thriller about a boy who flew into a rage when his girlfriend ended up pregnant and planned an elaborate murder-suicide scene in the woods behind his parents' garage but at the last minute chickened out of the suicide part and had to flee across the wilderness and ate slugs to stay alive, while police dogs followed, hot on his trail. This is a story about a careful boy who carefully purchased a moderately priced engagement ring and asked me if I wanted to take a ride on his brother's snowmobile across the lake to the island. He said he would make me cocoa. That's not as weird as it sounds, you know. The island was sort of our place.

"I know you can't drink or anything, so I didn't get any wine," he said, and I put on my jacket. It was cold out, enough so that your breath would freeze a little in the time between exhaling and the air actually leaving your mouth or your nose. I put on a red hat, with a little tuft of yarn on the top. When I bent down to grab the back of my boots, to sink my heels into the hollows I'd been trudging down all winter, it felt strange, like something was already changing the way my body moved, the way I stooped.

"I'll get an abortion," I said. It was the first time I had said those words out loud.

"It'll be okay," he said, and he ushered me toward the garage. "You'll see, Taylor. I promise."

NOW

Joey pushes his way past the foot of the bed, running into my shoulder as he goes by. My phone almost drops to the floor. "Joey," I say to his retreating back. "I don't know what you want."

He shakes his stupid hair out of his eyes. He's so tough, so full of bravado, this kid, and any girl can see the fragile center of him playing around with the idea of getting broken, just because. He's like a cold deep lake, sharp rock bottom visible. Scott was the kind of lake that has sturdy docks and patches of lily pads, a pleasant place to swim where you probably wouldn't drown. He was only nineteen, but inside he was at least forty, all safe and sensible. *Is. Scott is.*

"My brother didn't drive like that" is all Joey will say, and he gives his hair another shake and stalks off, toward the vending machines or some other place where he wants to be alone. His brother didn't drive like that. *Like that* meaning fast, reckless even. Out of control.

I sigh. I would like something from the vending machine, maybe. I can't tell if I should eat every couple of minutes or if I should never eat again. The nausea. I slide my phone back into my pocket and follow him.

"Joey, listen." His shoulders are narrow beneath his black jacket, some kind of skinny canvas thing like a mechanic would wear, faded patches, ragged edges. He wears skinny jeans, too, and the kid is like nothing but a nervous wiry mess. He punches the letters and numbers and waits, metal coiling slowly, for his dill pickle chips to fall into the bottom of the machine.

"Can we—can we talk about it?" It occurs to me then that I have nothing to say, no plan for what to tell him. I have no excuse.

Joey is forcing himself to stay put, keeping himself from running away from me. He wants to fight me but he doesn't want to win. His fingers fumble with the top of the shiny bag.

"You're going to end up with chips everywhere." I take it from him and pull the top open carefully. "Have you ever done that?" I try to smile. "I have. My mom always buys the big box with the two bags. They make them so hard to open."

"My mom gets the grocery store brand," he says, and of course I know this. I've spent hours on his family's couch sharing chips and sour cream dip. With Joey at times, in fact. He takes a deep breath. "Scott didn't want to marry you," he says.

I breathe, too, and he twists the bag around toward me,

the pickle smell wafting out of the wide mouth —the greasy invitation that, for the first time in weeks, makes me feel honestly hungry, with no hesitant swirl along for the ride. I reach for one, and I take several.

"It's okay." I crunch down on a potato chip, talking with my mouth full. "I didn't want to marry him either."

But I didn't mean to almost kill him. I mean, I'm almost certain.

THEN

The first time we went to the island, it's funny to think of it, really. It was summer, and it was hot, and I didn't know how to swim. That's stupid, right? I live in the land of 10,000 lakes or whatever, and I didn't know how to swim. It was Mary Ellen's fault, really. She was my counselor when I was a kid and I got chosen to go to this science camp for girls on Arrowhead Lake, an abandoned mine-turned-swimming beach. Mary Ellen knew all the really scary stories about that old mine pit, like have you heard the one about the ghost of Otto Jarvi and the Hanging Shack? All the girls held hands around the fire and giggle-screamed while Mary Ellen told us about the ghost of his ill-fated daughter, Petra Jarvi, who grabbed hold of the ankles of girls if they jumped off the end of the dock.

Mary Ellen said that Petra Jarvi took one eleven-year-old girl every eleven years to keep for her own in the depths of the old iron mine, and this was the year.

I was eleven. I refused to put one toe in the water after that.

So Scott had this little canoe, which is not as romantic as a little rowboat, and I told him so. It was our first date, and he sat behind me to paddle and steer. "If this were a rowboat you could face me, with your hands on two oars, and you could row me all the way around the lake while singing sweetly," I said. I could be so brave, since I couldn't see his face. I pretended to sit all prim in the bow of his canoe, wearing the stiff life preserver he insisted I wear, and to be truthful I was so glad he did because like I said, I couldn't swim. The canoe wobbled beneath us and I put my hands down on the sides. "Islands are overrated," I said, but he insisted.

He had some kind of alcohol, I can't remember what it was, some stupid bottle he'd stolen from his aunt or his grandma or something, but I remember he gave me this plastic cup, and he was really protective of how much I drank, like he rationed it out so I wouldn't get very drunk. He seemed so harmless.

Harmless. That's just what he was. *Is.*

So the snowmobile ride to the island was not completely unexpected, though it pretty much made it impossible to go through with my plans for the evening, which had been to break up with him. I hadn't quite decided on what to do about the other thing, but it seemed clear all of a sudden that this was something I wanted some space to figure out, on my own.

He drove us out to the island and I rode on the back, my arms loosely around the waist of his puffy down parka. We didn't wear helmets, which is something that people would later point out with a sad sort of pursed-lip pity, but it was the one safety measure Scott didn't believe in. It was because of some cousin of his who got into a motorcycle crash and the doctor told him that if he'd had a helmet on, he would have died. I don't know how many doctors are going around telling people that, but from the looks of the traumatic brain injury ward in Scott's hospital alone, doctors *should* be telling people to walk around wearing a helmet at all times, night and day. Anyway, he drove slowly, and we made it out there without incident, though Scott pointed out several dangers along the way, including the ridges made by people driving out here with plows on their trucks or ATVs. "You hit one of those going fast enough and your machine will crunch up like a pop can," he said. I remember that.

NOW

My face is pretty badass, even in the weird yellow light of the hospital bathroom. The toilet is close to the little sink, and I have to sit sort of tilted to one side to keep out of the way of the stainless steel stability bar. On the wall beneath the toilet paper hangs a little chain with a red plastic disc on the end. *Pull for nurse assistance.* My fingers idly flip the little disc, spin it. I wonder how the nurse would assist me, if I pulled. Me here, with my pants around my ankles and my split lip and my guilt.

I stand and flush, even though I can't remember if I peed or not. My head is foggy, and my face is terrible, and the water that runs from the tap is icy cold. I pool a little in my palms and think about splashing it onto my face, but it seems like too much work and I let it go, down the drain. Like my life. Oh, the melodrama, right? I stare again at my wrecked face and try to remember what happened, right before the crunch.

"The ice ridge." My voice is husky, and I wonder what would happen if I stayed in this bathroom all night talking to myself. It sounds like I smoke a pack a day, but I haven't had a cigarette since last Tuesday, when Dani made me stop. Scott would be so happy, since he always hated the smoking thing, and I wonder if that's why I did it. It was Joey who got me started, actually—the realization makes me a little uncomfortable. I squint at myself in the mirror, baring my teeth in a grimace. Do they look whiter? Do I look pregnant?

I read an article once about how if you look into a mirror in dim light and stare at yourself for some crazy amount of time, you'll start to hallucinate. Your face will turn into something else entirely, a demon or something. It happens to everyone, I guess, everyone who tries it. I tried it once, in my mom's bathroom, at midnight just to make it creepier. I guess I overestimated my tolerance for creepy shit, though, because after a couple of minutes something strange and taffy-like happened to my chin and then my forehead, and they kind of stretched out for a second like I was some kind of weird science experiment, and I freaked out. I was all alone, my mom out of town, and I didn't want to be a monster. I couldn't get my heart to stop racing for the longest time.

The light is plenty bright in this sterile little closet, but I don't have to look long before my own image repulses me.

THEN

Dani. I told her first, of course, way back when I peed on the stick and the little line said MOMMY despite all Scott's precautions. I don't know what I'd do without Dani, but that's the thing, right? That's the best friend thing. I mean, it used to be we were this little trio: Taylor-and-Dani-and-Evelyn. But Evie got too cool for us and joined the girls who decided Sterling Creek needed a lacrosse team and a Wannabe Ivy League Club or some stupid thing like that, and then it was just me and Dani, the Trashy League Club or something equally stupid like that. We weren't really trashy, but you know. My mom is a receptionist for a therapist who works with troubled teens in the foster care system, and my dad skipped town while I was hovering somewhere between the zygote and embryo stage. Dani's moms own a sleepy little yarn store just off Sterling Creek's thriving Main Street shopping district. Neither one of us will be going to Harvard when we graduate without some kind of miracle. Not this particular kind of miracle, in case that's not clear.

She didn't speak, not right away. For all her perky looks and loud cheerleader yells—her pink nail polish and shiny black ponytail like a perfect pendulum—Dani knows how to be quiet. We were cocooned in her little handmade loft bed, painted by her mom Janie to look like an old gnarled tree, with a green cloth canopy of leaves hand-sewn by Fran. Heaped behind Dani was a pile of plush spiders she's collected since she was two years old and arrived in Sterling Creek from an orphanage in Nepal, clinging to Neep—the oldest, rattiest spider of the bunch.

"Options," she said at last. "Do you want to hear them?" She held out her arms and I collapsed into her embrace, crying in complete silence for longer than I thought possible.

"My mom," I gasped, in between sobs, "will kill me."

Dani held me impossibly tight. "Let her even try," she said.

NOW

Sitting in this hospital, waiting in uncertainty, makes time go all funny. It rewinds and fast-forwards at the whim of something unseen. So you want to hear something weird?

I can see him sometimes, and he's always a boy, always with those wide, impossibly sweet blue eyes. Just like Scott. He's beautiful, but his face has that needy baby look. Hungry, like he would devour me whole.

And what if he did? That's stupid. But seriously, that's what babies do to people. What if I have this baby and it devours everything I am, all I could be or could have been? Am I a mother? That seems so abstract. And then there are the things that really scare me, the little phrases that fall out of my mouth, the tiny cruelties that remind me of the kind of mother I could become.

I'm getting an abortion. It's the right thing to do, especially now. I was about to break up with him. But the weird thing, you know, the weird thing is this other part, this other scene in the fast forward. I can imagine myself holding him out in offering, a blanket-wrapped bundle, all soft and blinking and needy and alive. This weird part of me wants to give this baby to them—to Understanding Emily and Angry Joey and to Scott's mom and dad with their wounded eyes and their fluttery hands. A consolation prize. Here is a part of your son I didn't ruin. Here is a part to help you move on.

THEN

He wasn't my first choice, not in the beginning. And I wasn't his. After school most days in the winter, Dani and I would go skating. Even on the coldest days, we walked there and back together, our cheap vinyl skates tied by their laces and looped over our shoulders. We wore long floppy mittens with ice chunks clinging to them from when we fell, or pretended to fall, giggling and helpless into the snow banks that surrounded the "girls' rink" adjacent to the hockey rink, where the boys who were the reason for us being there in the first place circled fast, snapping their sticks against the ice like weapons.

Dani could whistle with her fingers between her teeth, and she could skate fast right up to the edge and stop with a spray of snow against our side of the wooden boards that contained the boys. The shrill call would cut through the sound of their skates scraping across the ice and the pucks clanging off the metal pipes that surrounded the net. Sometimes, not often, they would whistle back, and once the whole group of boys skated over and leaned against the edge and talked to us, but they were mostly juniors and seniors, and we were still ninth graders stuck in the dregs of junior high, even though every other school in the world put the freshmen in the high school. Basically, all we did was a lot of giggling. Dani said it was hard to be sexy when we were wearing so much clothing, so after that we started sneaking out of our houses without our snow pants on, our skinny jeans clinging to our skinny legs. Still, the boys barely looked. They circled the rink like sharks and flipped their wrist shots over and over, even though we waited for hours, hoping they would head into the warming shack for a break. All our plans for seduction seemed to revolve around the warming shack.

I had my eye on this redhead we called Ron Weasley, even though his real name was Kenny or Denny or something like that. There was no particular reason why I settled on him to be the object of my high school hockey player fantasies, other than I liked the way his hair curled up when he was sweaty, and he almost never spit on the ice—a habit I found disgusting. He was a senior and obviously safe because he was completely unavailable.

Scott wasn't looking for me—one of those annoying, skinny-legged freshman girls hanging around the warming shack all winter long—but he did have a blister starting on one foot, and he knew immediately from the feel of it that if he did not venture into the shack and change something about the way his sock was bunched up against his heel, he would end up with a blister that would keep him off the ice for a week or more. Dani and I chased him in, asking his name, telling him he had ugly feet. "Oh my god!" squealed Dani, jumping up on her toe-picks, sticking them into the black rubber mats on the floor. "Your toes are hairy!"

"Like a hobbit," I said, and that's when he looked at me for the first time.

He used to snuggle up to me sometimes, like when we went to a movie or sat around the fire on the island, and I would think he was leaning in to say something incredibly sweet in my ear—he did that, too, sometimes. Anyway, he would lean in and then he would whisper in my ear, he'd go "Hobbit toes!", and that unstoppable kind of laughter would steal over me until I collapsed against him, tears trapped in my eyelashes, warm and content.

NOW

"Will he remember the accident?" The words spill out of my mouth when Scott's doctor approaches us in the waiting room. "Will he remember what happened?"

The doctor squares her shoulders, pulls herself together. "He's no longer receiving medication to keep him in the coma," she says. She suggests I talk to him, or read to him, anything to have the familiar voices of his loved ones calling him back. "When Scott wakes, he might need us to help him find his place again. Memory is a complex process."

Tell me about it.

THEN

I wasn't allowed to see Scott. Technically. Anyway, I wasn't allowed to visit him in St. Cloud while he was living on his own for college. I accused my mom of being controlling, told her she couldn't control love. I slammed my bedroom door.

"That's what the kids are calling it these days," said my mom's boyfriend-of-the-month with an awful wink, and Mom repeated the rule that Scott and I could only see each other when he was at "home." Meaning, of course, his parents' home. "Supervised," she said. "At all times."

Scott was the kind of guy who never broke any rules. It turned me into the kind of girl who wanted to corrupt him, somehow. I did love him, that's important to know. I loved his voice, I loved his smile, I loved his eyes—the way they looked at me like I mattered. I loved sitting beside him on his parents' couch, even when we watched hockey. Scott explained all the rules of the game with patience and enthusiasm and I couldn't help seeing the sport in a new light, something we could share.

He didn't play for St. Cloud State, but during his sophomore year he did play defense on an intramural team, and Dani covered for me once a week so I could drive down and watch him play. My mom would have killed me if she found out, but luckily she never followed through on her threat of dropping by the public library to check on me. I watched him from an empty place in the stands, his new friends still strangers to me, his long easy strides building a slow sort of speed as he crossed the ice. I cheered for him, unabashedly, remembering the long years of leaning on the boards from the figure skating rink. He was my boyfriend. He was sweet to me.

Like I said, too, we were careful.

NOW

There's no change, but at least Scott is stable. In serious condition, which is a significantly more positive outlook than critical. Emily offers to drive me home, and I don't want to go, but it's not really an option to stay. This situation has moved beyond the point of staying awake through to the end, and I might as well rest in my own bed. I feel like a liar, like I'm coming home late from a party I didn't have permission to attend, instead of arriving home from the hospital after surviving a really scary snowmobile crash that left my boyfriend in critical condition. Serious condition. At least nobody has noticed I'm pregnant.

My mom came to the hospital, but I wouldn't leave with her. I wish she'd stayed, but I understand, I guess. She has to work in the morning and stuff. It's just that ... wouldn't she want Scott's parents to be there for comfort if it had been the other way around? If I had been the one in the coma?

If I had been. I think I should have been. I can't remember if I was sitting in front or in back, but I should have been the one to hit the ice because I know it had to have been my fault we crashed. Scott was such a careful driver.

My mom is... well, she's difficult to understand, even for me sometimes. She's the kind of person I always sort of think I've got all rationalized in my head, like I understand where she's coming from, and then she surprises me, attacks me somewhere I don't even know I have feelings. I know she loves me. I hope she's sleeping.

Emily insists on accompanying me to the front door, and I fumble with my keys, trying to figure out if my confusion is mere clumsiness or head injury. I do have a mild concussion. My thinking is weird, but I'm not sure if it's shock or what. My memory has a skip in it, like a rock flipped over the surface of the lake; I have gaps.

The ice ridge.

My fingers shake, and the door swings open before I can get my key in the lock. My mother, wearing a hoodie and yoga pants. So on her way to bed but not sleeping yet. There's one light on in the entryway, and my mom smiles at Understanding Emily, her hair softly backlit. Her face in shadow, mostly.

"Is she doing okay?" Her concern is real, but her hands make me flinch, coming so close to my face. "My poor baby." She touches the bridge of my nose and even my split lip, but I hold myself still and act normal. Emily smiles, her eyes oblivious.

"Your glasses are bent," my mom says, like that's the most important thing here.

"She needs some sleep, but you should wake her every so often to check on her because of the concussion." Emily presses herself tightly up to me, her arms squeezing tight. "Call me if you need me," she says, and then squeezes again. "He's going to be okay, Taylor, I can feel it."

I'm not a hugger. I feel my arms come up and circle around her, feel them clinging strangely, someone else's arms. Desperate arms. I step back, but she pulls me even closer. "You're just like my sister already," says Emily, and I can't breathe. "Get some sleep, and I'll call you tomorrow morning."

"Or if anything changes," I say. Like if Scott wakes up and remembers everything. Even the parts I don't.

Her eyes are so warm, so loving. "I'll call you if anything changes," she promises.

THEN

The island was special. It carried the weight of so many firsts.

Scott liked to build fires, to be an architect and build them like these perfect structures. He was a fire designer, setting his tinder up just so, little chips of wood with the edges all curled up and shredded in a perfect little flammable pile. This guy Cody from the hockey team—his dad was a big-time survivalist dude, and they lived out in the woods all crazy and wild—he showed Scott once how to start the fire with a cotton ball dipped in Vaseline. He gave Scott a flint and a little piece of steel on a loop of parachute cord. Scott couldn't quite manage to get the sparks to catch, though, and I got tired of watching. I reached for the flint. "Let me try."

It was kind of amazing, if you want to know the truth, the way it felt to make a shower of sparks fly from the back of the knife. They rained down on the little cotton ball until it caught, turning into a round glow before a little orange flame burst up from the top, and I skewered it with a sharp chunk of kindling and moved it into the little center of the structure Scott built. It went up in a fury of hot flames, and I felt the warmth climb up my body.

You could come close to falling in love with anyone sitting around a well-constructed fire on a beautiful summer night. Close was all that really mattered, and Scott pulled me into his lap in one of the rickety lawn chairs he and his friends kept on the island, stashed in the weeds. We were both hot, from the fire and from our own daring. I remember that heat sometimes, the searing ecstasy of his mouth perhaps —it should always be easy as that to fall in love with the person you're wondering if you are in love with. Sit beside a fire and climb into their lap and everything else falls away.

We went to the island for many reasons, and we went there often. In summer, Scott paddled the little canoe while I gripped the sides and tried to keep breathing. In the winter we drove across on Joey's snowmobile, but a lot of times it was too cold to stay long. Once we built a snowman family and dressed them up like they were marooned on a tropical island. They waved their little stick arms for help, and Scott and I laughed ourselves into a slushy puddle of greedy mouths and cold hands and shuddery breath.

The island was a place for memories.

NOW

This snow is the kind that snaps against the window pane in grainy waves, carried by the fiercely gusting winds that rock the corners of the old house. I like weather that reminds me how lucky I am to have shelter.

My bed is lumpy. This is nothing new; I think the mattress has needed replacing since before I inherited this bed from some other poor person who brought it to Goodwill. Scott and I have had sex on this bed on four separate occasions, as if that matters. As if there's any reason on earth for me to be thinking about that right now. God, what is wrong with me?

I fold my hands over my abdomen, and I try to determine if there has been any change in my size or shape. I don't think so, though I can feel some of the changes in my hips, in the way my body fits together at the joints. I've lost two pounds since that day I peed on the shoplifted stick in the drug store bathroom. No change, not really, but I push my stomach out until it rounds beneath the sheet, beneath my hands. If I let this baby stay, what will happen to me?

I think about the dumbest things. Like about how people will look at me. That people will be able to see, in one glance, what I've done. It isn't cool, the way girls have to walk around for nine months plus whatever else with this scarlet letter or whatever, fucking *advertising* that we had sex. And whatever. So you know what? I *liked* having sex with Scott. I slide my hands a little lower. How dumb is it that I'm thinking about having sex with him and he's maybe not even thinking at all? He's lying there in a vegetative state or something, and everyone's just waiting to see what will happen, what his brain will be like, what he'll remember, and I'm busy thinking about how it used to make me smile when he would hold me close enough that I could feel him wanting me.

I was giving this up, remember? *I was about to break up with you.* How can I be lying here thinking about all the times he sat pressed up against me on the seat of the snowmobile. It's the fire, those fires he was always starting. *Was?* I can't let him shift into past tense. I slide up to a seated position in the bed, my breath hitching in my chest a little. I put my hands where I can see them. I was about to break up with him. I remember the reason.

I pull my knees up close, wrapping my arms around my shins. I'll get an abortion. I have to find a way. I get to choose because it's my scarlet letter, and it's not only that. What if he's different? What if he's broken? What kind of father could he be?

He needs to wake up. I hate it that he left me all alone with all of this.

THEN

Scott loved candy. It was funny at first because it was like his hidden weakness. The door pocket on the driver's side of his truck was filled with candy wrappers. Once, when things were new between us, I teased him that I wasn't sweet enough for him, and he didn't say a word. He leaned over and licked me, from the lowest dip of my scooped-neck tank top right up my neck and the bottom of my ear and all the way up to my temple, where he placed a little surprise of a kiss.

"Gross!" I pushed him away and wiped my hand across my cheek, all dramatic. "Sweetness germs!"

After that he called me Sweetness whenever he was teasing me, and I know that sounds the lamest of the lame of all things, but it made me feel special to hear him say it, and sometimes he still surprised me by licking some random exposed bit of me, eliciting a shriek and spreading those good old sweetness germs.

NOW

I bring candy to the hospital, lots of different kinds but mostly the sour chewy varieties, which is what he liked best. Likes best. The nurse is a tall black woman with tightly braided hair, and she smiles when she says she'll be working this shift all week. Her name is Lydia, and she holds my face in her hands for a moment, examining my injuries. She clicks her tongue. "Stupid snowmobiles," she says.

She doesn't have much time, but she talks to me while she checks Scott's vitals and records some notes into the computer. "He might be able to smell the candy," she says, "if you unwrap it and hold it by his nose." She stands up from the rolling stool and reaches over to adjust some tubing leading into my boyfriend's arm. My boyfriend. I can't even think that without wondering. What will he remember? "Just talk to him, Taylor." Lydia squeezes me in a hug—

not usually my thing, but I don't fight it, don't even pull back from it like I would have for anyone else—and then she sets Scott's chart back on the wall at the foot of his bed and exits the room on silent white sneakers.

"Hey, Scott. It's me, Taylor." My voice feels faint and far-away, but in my ears, in the strange silence of the room, it sounds abnormally loud. It's so awkward, talking to what feels like an empty room. They've taken him off the ventilator, so there's no real machine noise in the room except for occasional beeps of the IV or the automatic blood pressure cuff. What can I say into this hush, into those still ears on the side of that pale, shaven head, mostly hidden under bandages and a knit hat. "Nice hat you've got there," I say, lowering my voice because my god, if anyone hears me they'll think I'm cognitively impaired. "I suppose a stupid hat on your stupidly smashed-up head is as good a place to start as any." I pull up a chair. "Lydia said you might be able to smell, too, so I brought some of your favorite candies, and I . . . I'm going to hold them under your nose." I unwrap a piece of salt water taffy and hold it out. Not exactly under his nose—that doesn't seem dignified—but close enough so that he could probably smell it. If he can smell things. "Um. So can you smell things? Look. This is weird, you know? Talking to you like this. There are probably a lot of things I would say to you if I thought there was no way in hell you were actually hearing me. And there are things I could say if I thought for certain that you were hearing me, especially if I knew that nobody else could hear. But this . . . it's a weird limbo, you know? And I'm all tongue-tied."

I have to look at him in little pieces, not all at once. The dark bruise around his eye, fading into purple and blue on the edges, the spiky bits of stubble on the edge of his jawline where the nurse didn't shave him close enough. The soft curve of his fingernails against the white sheets. The steady rise and fall of his chest, moving now without the aid of a machine.

"I want you to wake up so we can talk about some pretty serious stuff." I pop the candy into my mouth and chew, my mouth filling with saliva that I have to slurp indelicately to avoid drooling. God, I can't even have a serious conversation with a comatose person without messing it up. "I mean, like, I need to know if you remember what happened, and how it happened, or who did it or why. And I need to tell you about the ring and what I'm thinking about with the one thing. You know I can't marry you, Scott, and I know you don't even want that. What was that, anyway? How did you expect me to feel?"

I've been keeping the ring in my pocket because I can't bear to wear it, but I feel like it should be nearby in case he wakes up. I pull it out and stare at it, settled on the palm of my left hand. It's not the engagement ring I'd choose for myself, but then again I've always kind of thought that was weird, that you'd go along with a boy and say, spend this much money on me. This is what I'm worth, if you want to keep my heart.

"You don't have to be here."

I startle at the angry voice coming from the doorway, and the ring bounces off the tile floor and rolls out of sight.

"Joey, seriously. What's your issue?" Did he see the ring? I can't crawl under the bed right now and search for it unless I'm willing to have a witness, and a hostile one at that. "I'm aware that I don't *have* to be here. I walked four blocks in the middle of winter and froze my tail off waiting at the bus stop for almost an hour, then had to ride all the way over to the community college and the mall before the stupid bus finally looped back over to the hospital. All that to get here. To sit here, to have you treat me like dirt because you're mad at your brother."

Joey's wearing the same jeans, the same jacket. He walks like someone who's slept in a waiting room. "I'm not mad at Scott," he says, muttering under his breath.

"You're mad at me, then? For what? For existing? For not being there instead of him?"

He paces the space, twisting all the air in the room about himself. "My brother will never be the same," he says. "He may not ever be able to speak, to walk, to feed himself. And I *know*, Taylor. No fucking way my brother was driving that snowmobile. He's never wrecked in his life." Each of his words is a sharp stone, hurting us both.

"We shouldn't be doing this, not in front of Scott," I say. Lydia said he might be able to smell. He might be able to hear. "Help me talk to him, Joey." Maybe we can do this instead. My mouth is dry. "Let's bring him back."

"You did this," he says. His finger jabs at the air between us and then at the bed. At Scott. "This is your fault."

I unwrap a caramel and start from the beginning.

THEN

(TO JOEY)

Grave Lake, it was called, and I worried about the implications of that name from day one. I didn't know how to swim, but it wasn't that. I took a photo of him on the path to Grave Lake, and I put one of those stupid filters on it, see? Anyway, look—he was so gorgeous and vulnerable and young. In this photo, he looks like someone who might take a risk. Someone who might find himself saying things like, "Bet on yourself!" after spending a week in the woods with only a knife and his little fire-starter. Someone who might follow his heart.

I remember that comment you posted when Scott made this his profile photo. You were teasing him about how he looked so tough but probably whined about the mosquitos for the rest of the hike. I remember how I wished you'd been wrong.

There was beauty, though, moments where Scott really was the perfect boyfriend. You're probably familiar with the sandbar, the way the fireflies came out on shore and you could float on your stomach with your hands in the sand and try to catch the pattern of blinking lights, to make sense of its coded urgency.

NOW

I'm surprised that Joey listens, that he takes my invitation. His hands are stuffed into the chest pockets of his jacket, his expression dark, but he keeps his eyes focused on Scott, on the rise and fall of his chest going solo on the whole breathing gig.

"I remember that picture," he says, still spitting the words between his teeth. "Him standing there like a hero." A dark laugh escapes him. "And now look at him."

"Yeah." I shift my body closer to the bed, closer to Scott's face, looking for movement. Buying myself time. "This isn't my fault." My shoulders, my chest, everything shakes, even my lungs seem shaky, like I can't get enough to breathe. "I didn't want this."

"You think it's that easy? *I didn't want this so make it go away.* It doesn't work that way, Taylor."

I'm aware it doesn't work that way. I don't need him lecturing me about the way the world works. I need to find my freaking engagement ring off the floor of this hospital room so I can leave before my ex-boyfriend's angry little brother tries to avenge his brother's death by—my god, I have to stop killing Scott in my head. I didn't kill him. I never wanted that.

I have this image, in my head, and I'm not really sure where it comes from but it's so vivid—this image I think must be a memory until it suddenly can't be. My jacket, puffy and pink, the snow ridge in front of me, the scramble of the collision, and I can see myself looking down, looking at my abdomen as though from a distance, the spill of blood against the snow. An image of Scott, holding my hand as I die.

And that's it. That's the only image I can bring up in my head about the crash, that and the noise of Scott's skull against the ice, but obviously this memory isn't real and for all I know neither is the sound. I flew free of the machine and landed in deep snow. How can we both be in the same crash, and he's the one in a coma, while I'm fine beyond a headache and a fuzzy memory. The doctors basically waved a light in my eyes a few times and told me to stay home from school a couple of days, while Scott is lying here unresponsive, barely breathing on his own. I didn't tell anyone at the hospital I was pregnant.

"I have a story too, then," says Joey, and his bones seem to reanimate with a new kind of solidity, less rage and more—something. I don't have the word. Something makes me sit up and look at him differently, to see more than Scott's dangerously broken little brother. "It's about Scott, and it's about why I know you were driving that snowmobile."

I might have been driving. I don't remember. They had me talk with the psychologist that once, but there's all the insurance stuff to deal with, so I don't know.

Joey clears his throat. "Okay. I'm not a writer, so, not like you. You know they say all writers are good liars." He looks up, clears his throat again, but when he starts to speak, all that preamble disappears. "Back when Scott and I were kids, we'd go out in the woods and shoot at rabbits. We had our pistols from Dad in our holsters and spent the days having sharp-shooting contests, trying to hit sticks and chunks of dirt and ice floating down the river. Scott was better than me at the range. I can't remember beating him a single time with a backstop and a target. But try and get him to shoot at something floating on the water or stuck in the ice and even when the banks were high he would go on about ricochets and safety until he missed at least half of his chances to shoot."

He glares at me, but I get it. I wish I had someone else to blame, too.

"He wouldn't even let me hold the gun until I could recite the five rules of firearm safety," I say. My face twists up into a smile, and I know it's one of the things I teased him about but also one of the things I was drawn to. Scott always had the safety on. I didn't have to stop and read every facial expression, every movement. I trusted him. "I don't remember the crash."

Joey only nods. "That's what the police said."

"I swear it's the truth." I take a bottle of sunscreen out of my purse and squirt a little bit on Scott's lifeless hand, thinking maybe he'll remember this smell, this story. "I'm not a liar just because I write poetry, you know."

THEN

(TO JOEY, BLUSHING)

This is about the island, two summers ago. I shouldn't have been there. For one thing, my skin is fair, so I was basically setting myself up for skin cancer lying there in the sun all afternoon. But then there was my new bathing suit, the unsupervised beach, the way Scott's head rested on my stomach, I mean whatever, you get the idea. I knew I'd be dead if my mom found out, but I didn't care. It was a moment worth every consequence.

That was the first official date we'd had where we weren't exactly doing what we said we were going to be doing. I was fifteen, and my mom made it very clear that she was uncomfortable with the idea of me dating a boy who was nearly eighteen. "It's just a number," I told her, and she slapped me.

I mean, not that hard. Just hard enough to let me know that wasn't a sanctioned opinion.

So it was easier, with my mom, to sneak around and hope to not get caught. Anyway, we told her that we were going to a car show, of all things. I didn't even know what a car show was. I curled up against his side on the drive over to the lake, or at least as close as I could get in the front seat of his truck without taking off the stupid seat belt he insisted I wear. "Buckle up, it's the law," he would say, and he'd smile like such a geek when he said it. "You can't tame me!" I would always say, but then he'd laugh and I would fasten my belt and put my head on his shoulder and smile. He was my boyfriend. We were happy.

I fully admit that I was the one who pursued him. Ever since the moment he stumbled into that warming shack all unawares, focused only on the hot spot in his skate, your brother was a hunted man. "Pursued" might be putting it too kindly. You probably remember what pests we were. With Dani's help, I stalked your brother, online and off. Both Dani and I chat-messaged him relentlessly with stupid questions. We rode the activity bus (illegally, without parent permission slips properly on file!) over to the high school so we could hang around and talk Scott's ear off in the weight room, where, we'd discovered, nobody much cared that we were not high school students as long as we didn't actually try to mess around with the weights. And Scott was so good-natured about it, too. He let us prattle on about Doctor Who and Shakespeare and learning to play the ukulele, which we would pronounce very seriously with a Hawaiian pronunciation, and then we'd look down our noses for a long beat before simultaneously bursting into gales of laughter. He rolled his eyes (I miss those eyes so much) and focused on lifting and breathing and other hard-working type stuff that looked pretty damn impressive from our point of view, and, my god, he was a senior and nothing could happen.

But here it was, the summer before tenth grade, the super hot days at the end of summer when you're just relaxed enough to think you'll never be bored of summer but just bored enough to be the tiniest bit interested in school starting, and Scott was going to college in a month and I was going to high school for real, and Dani and I had plans to start a zine filled with poetry and Sharpie art and an entire section devoted to cool names for if we had a band.

Twice, Scott and I had met up with other girls and other boys, including Dani and the Ron Weasley boy from the hockey rink who turned out to be really nice but completely forgettable. Once we went to this movie thing that they projected on a huge screen in the park. People brought their dogs and blankets and coolers, and there were about a million mosquitoes and people talking all through the movie, including us. The second time was the Fourth of July, and we all went downtown to the street dance, where the city blocked off about half of Main Street and the area all around Sterling Lake and three bands played on makeshift stages at the far ends of each of the three branches of the T-shaped area. That night, there had been fireworks and more loud, giggly conversations.

But this time, we'd ditched our crowd of friends and instead of going to the car show like we'd told my mom, Scott took me across the lake in his canoe, and I brought along my new bikini. That was the moment, lying there on the beach on the island—the moment Scott fell in love with me. I swear, I could feel it happen. His head on my stomach, and his eyes closed, but I knew he was looking at me anyway. In whatever ways a boy can look at a girl. I was feeling pretty proud of myself for getting away with it all—with having a boyfriend before I turned sixteen, for one thing, and with convincing my mom we were going to a car show without even really knowing what a car show was, for another. *My boyfriend.* I said those words in my head, my elbows propped on my Hogwarts towel. There was sand everywhere. The whole island was made of it, except where it was rock. Sand and rock.

I kind of felt like that's what we were, Scott and me. Sand and rock. I'm the rock, of course. I didn't care if he was older than me, more experienced, whatever. I'm always stubbornly myself, and I always have been. It's why my mom and I never could sit in a room together for more than five minutes without at least one of us yelling.

I want you to know that. It's not my mom's fault, or not any more than half. It doesn't matter to this, to Scott, but somehow it matters to me, for whatever reason, what you think.

He was looking at me with his eyes closed, the sand trapped everywhere, and he started falling—I felt it happen. And it was exciting, you know? I was powerful and I liked the feeling. My boyfriend.

NOW

I put my head down on my arms, stretch out on the edge of the bed. *I was about to break up with you.*

"So you didn't love him, even back then. I knew it." Joey puts his hat back on and settles the brim low. "You paraded him around, so proud of your *boyfriend*, proud of your power over him, but I could see you weren't right for each other. I tried to tell him. We got into a huge fight over him buying you that ring."

"You're misinterpreting everything," I say. Of course I love Scott. He's my boyfriend. And even if he hadn't bought a ring, if I *had* actually broken up with him, I'd still love him. It's not like a person can spend every waking thought on another person for two years without a deep emotional connection. I lean closer to the bed, put my hand back on Scott's arm. He feels weird, animate and yet not, somehow, like a couch cushion in the shape of my boyfriend, his muscles strangely tense. "Scott." I speak up. "I love you, okay? I don't know what your idiot brother has against me, but I've been telling how you fell in love with me, and I think you should wake up and tell the other side. Tell Joey how I fell in love with you."

Joey makes a show of staring at Scott's still form for a good ten-count. "Looks like the jury's still out on that one," he says, standing up. "Anyway, *idiot brother* wants a hamburger."

I feel heat rush to my face. "Sorry, I—"

"Hungry? Café on the third floor?" The hat still obscures his eyes, but he jerks his head toward the door.

I remember the dill pickle potato chips. That was the last time I ate without feeling the nausea. The sudden thought of a thick cheeseburger with the grease running into the toasted edge of the bun … "Are you asking me to lunch?" I give Scott's cushiony arm another squeeze and stand up.

Joey scowls and folds his arms across his chest. "I don't like you in here alone with him, that's all," he says. "For all I know, you'll try to smother him with a pillow." He tries to keep his voice all growly and tough, but beneath it all I hear a quiet wavering, like the beginning of tears or laughter. Maybe both.

THEN

(TO JOEY)

It was true, you know. I was preoccupied with my ACT scores. Dani and I weren't in the Ivy League Club, so we had to make damn sure we could at least get into the Scholarship-to-a-state-school Club. My mom didn't go to college, and that's her own complicated story; I wasn't going to let her interfere with mine. I was applying to all the same places Dani did because we were best friends and we were going to have so much fun in college, you have no idea.

I had a hard time deciding what I wanted to be. I mean, I really wanted to be both a poet and a doctor. "Oh, like a pediatrician?" asked my guidance counselor. She smiled sweetly at me, like she knew I was too dumb for such a thing but would humor me for a while before letting me know about this great nursing aide program that would be "a great place to start out, and then you could work your way up!" But I sort of wanted to be a cardiologist. I liked the idea of fixing people's broken hearts—it seemed like the perfect blend of poetry and medicine. Dani would do art or art history or history or women's studies, she wasn't sure, and I was balancing the idea of double majoring pre-med and English. In any case, I was applying to St. Cloud, the U, and Mankato State, but the only way I'd be able to go is if my test scores were good enough to qualify me for the academic scholarships.

"I don't know why you're thinking of going somewhere other than St. Cloud," Scott said. He stirred a French fry into some disgusting blend of condiments and pouted.

"I don't know why I would choose my education based on proximity to a boy," I said, and I was only partly serious. It's not that I didn't want to go to the same school as him, but we were talking about almost a whole year away and a lot of things could happen.

"I don't know, you didn't seem to mind my *proximity* earlier." He kissed my cheek to keep it from sounding too slimy. That was the night it happened, I guess—was it homecoming weekend? In the stupid truck with most of our clothes on because it was too cold.

"Gross." I pushed Scott away, him smelling of mayo and ketchup or whatever. We always went to the Village Inn, like everyone else did when it was too cold to drive around anymore and nobody's parents were gone so we could have a place to hang out. We nursed our sugary coffees and flipped the little creamers with our fingertips and waited to be old enough to live in our own place. "I'm hungry, actually," I said and flagged the waiter down. "And not for those disgusting fries. You're going to buy me some cheesecake." I smiled at Scott, who stuck out his tongue.

"Anything for milady," he said, bowing his head. He was like that all the time, you know. Cute and playful. I took his hand, and he picked up mine and kissed it. He meant that, really. He would have done anything for me, anything at all.

NOW

Joey is absorbed. In his menu, in his phone, in the dark surface of his coffee. I've never seen someone pay so much attention to a hamburger. "Joey." This burger is good, but it's not that good. "What's going on in there?" I knock on the side of my own head.

"You're pregnant," he says at last. He's pale, and he sits back in his chair as though his rage has been all that was holding him upright until this moment, and now all the rage has somehow transformed into a mistier kind of confusion and shock, which shows on his face in broad strokes.

"Yeah." An eternity of silence follows. I stare at the brim of his cap until finally, when I've almost decided that he's been turned to stone by my condition, Joey speaks.

"His ridiculous plan was to marry you." He still won't look up, and he takes a wolfish bite of his burger.

I sigh. I take another bite too, and for a while it's only the two of us chewing, the conversation of a woman and her young granddaughter coming over the booth behind me. The greasy smell of the place is oddly comforting, and it keeps me hungry, keeps my stomach on an even keel. So that's what pregnancy is going to be, then? Eating greasy food in greasy places to keep from throwing up? Well, it could be worse.

"It wasn't that ridiculous," I say. "I mean, it was a viable option, but I was going to say no. I didn't ... I didn't get the chance." Joey doesn't answer, doesn't look at me.

I take another bite, and I'm mid-chew when the revolving door spins and a pair of police officers step into the hospital café. My mouth goes dry as a stone, grinding against the chunk of dust-dry hamburger bun. Did they find a clue at the scene of the crash? Did Scott wake up and remember something? I force my jaws to keep moving up and down. The blood spilling out of my belly as Scott held my hand ... the *crunch* ... whose hands were on the handlebars? Who was driving? Why does it matter so much? I reach for my water and force some of my mouthful down, enough to let me breathe a little easier, anyway.

"They're looking this way."

Joey spins in his seat and checks out the two cops by the door. He turns back, and now he actually looks me in the eye. "Got something to hide?"

"Funny." I stick my tongue out, but he's not Scott. He just gives me that dark and wounded look before his eyes sink back to his plate.

"I wasn't joking," he says.

63

The two officers of the law nod to the girl who smiles and hands them menus. I try not to stare as they make their way to the spot behind Joey. The booth we're in wiggles a little while they settle in, and the woman cop orders coffee. The man asks for water without ice. This bit of fussiness annoys me.

"Come on, Joey. We're both upset." I pick at the kettle chips on my plate, sucking the salt off my fingers. I wish his accusations didn't push me in the direction of thoughts that I'm afraid to think.

"Upset." He pulls the brim of his hat down lower. "Wow, thanks for that word, Taylor, that's great. You're really helping me express my feelings about this exquisitely fucked-up situation. Really helping me heal."

"Grieving, then," I say. "There's a twelve-step process, I think."

He snorts. "That's for alcoholics, you dumbass."

I can't help it. I laugh at the absurdity of all of this, and then I can't stop—these shuddering breaths of stupid laughter. The cop facing me looks up, her eyes keen. I'm making a scene. I put my hand over my mouth, but my whole body shakes. The booth wiggles beneath us.

Joey twists in his seat, moving to face the cops, to include them in our discussion. "Can you grieve for someone who isn't dead?" he says. He holds up his phone, flips through five or six tabs on his browser, reads out possible long-term outcomes of traumatic brain injuries. I no longer find anything funny. "My brother could end up living the rest of his life in a persistent vegetative state," he says. "He could be paralyzed, or he could suffer from vertigo, along with impulsive behavior, for the rest of his life, incapable of walking down a city street without the danger of being arrested on suspicion of being on drugs or inebriated." The cops exchange a look, but the woman only offers a sympathetic look and a nod.

"Joey, come on. Let's take a walk." My hands are shaking, and I pull out a twenty and put it on the table to cover our burgers. I smile back at the woman. "His brother," I say softly. "Snowmobile accident." They know the story; I can see the recognition in their eyes.

"It wasn't an accident," says Joey, and he reaches out for the cop's shirt sleeve. The cop shifts in his seat to maintain distance, and I pull Joey back by his own shirt. "She's the one who was driving," he adds, but he calms down, his attention back on his phone, the brim of his hat once again settled low and sullen.

"You're the girlfriend, then?" says the woman, and her eyes have that earlier keenness. "What do you mean, 'it wasn't an accident'?"

I shake my head. "I don't remember the crash."

She looks disappointed. "You're the one the reporter was looking for."

THEN

(TO JOEY)

So right after my mom caught us not going to the car show, Scott and I had our first fight. Maybe it was my sunburn that gave me away, the sand in my sheets or in the bottom of the shower. Maybe it was my friends; maybe they gave too many details when they lied for me. Maybe it was *her* friends—spies who didn't see me at the show, or who did see me in a tipsy canoe with a boy three years my senior. Probably it was the fact that I still didn't really know what a car show was when Scott dropped me off at home that evening, and the fact that I was still a little shaky with the sun and the sand and the falling in love, when she met me at the door to smell my breath for alcohol and wait for me to slip up in a lie.

When I'm telling you this, it feels like you're seeing me

differently, you know? Like I'm a girl whose mom abused her, I suppose. At least that's how Scott saw it, which is why we fought. I don't know. It's not like she was hitting me. I mean, besides an occasional slap across the face because I can be a real smartass. And look, I know parents shouldn't hit their kids, like ever. I know that, and I'm not saying she's perfect, but I am saying there's more nuance to things than you know.

The morning after our escapade to the island, Scott came over to pick me up. We were really going out with friends that time. We were on our way to a picnic and Frisbee golf match at the park near Sterling Lake. When Scott pulled up, Mom ran right out to the car and opened the driver's door before Scott could even take off his seat belt. She stood there loudly berating him in front of the whole world. I stepped into a pair of flip-flops by the door and chased down the driveway after her.

"Mom, what the hell?" I grabbed for her arm, which was greasy with sunscreen.

"You lying piece of trash." She yelled at me and shook me off—maybe she pushed me, I don't know. I told Scott I tripped on my stupid flimsy shoes, and that might be the truth, but I don't really know. I lost my balance and fell to the driveway, skinned my elbow and bruised my hip. She cried when she saw the blood and instantly we had apologies, a string of explanations, attempts at hugging, endless explanations—she'd been so worried, I could have been killed, what if she'd died of a heart attack and nobody knew where I was? She was stressed, and I had lied to her. I was embarrassed, though.

Anyway, so she tried to hug me, and I shrugged her off, and she tried to say Scott and I couldn't possibly go on our picnic, but he was still sitting there, buckled into his stupid seat belt, his face all stony and hard. "Mom, seriously, I'm not a little kid." I hopped into the passenger seat and rolled down my window as Scott drove away. "You can ground me when I get home," I shouted. She folded her arms.

See, though? Scott didn't wait for me to buckle my seat belt before he spun tires getting out of my mom's driveway. He wasn't always Mr. Safety, not when he was angry. It was tense for like three blocks, and we didn't talk. Scott slammed on the brakes at each stop sign and then accelerated equally aggressively when crossing each intersection. Finally, he pulled to a stop and parked, stomping on the emergency brake.

"Why are you freaking out?" I said. I mean, sure, my mom yelled at him, but she yells at everybody—at the kids at the beach who are throwing stones, at the people letting their dogs run in the park without a leash. And anyway, it wasn't like she was his mom. "It's fine, honestly. I'll deal with her when I get home." I reached for his hand, but he pushed it away—not angrily, but like my hand was a sad moth in the window and he was setting it free.

"I'm not freaking out. Taylor, that was not okay." He put both hands on the steering wheel.

I sat there for like a minute without saying anything, pulling the shoulder strap of my seat belt over me and then letting it retract, again and again.

"What do you want me to say?" I didn't really understand what was making him so angry—me or my mom.

"She can't treat you like that," he said. He was still gripping the wheel, still looking straight ahead with his jaws clenched tight. "I want you to tell me she's never acted like that before, that you're traumatized a little by that, maybe, or at least upset about what just happened."

We got caught, that's what happened. "I'm not sure how you expected her to respond."

NOW

When the police officer mentions the reporter, all I can think about is the ring I left lying on Scott's hospital room floor. I picture all kinds of stupid scenes out of movies and TV shows, the badass investigative reporter throwing me curveball questions that will somehow crack my façade, pull repressed memories out of my psyche like candy from a piñata. Joey walks away from the hospital with a purpose, and I follow because I have a small suspicion that he may be walking to the gas station to buy some cigarettes, and if he does, I'm going to make him give me one.

"Your mom sounds like a piece of work," Joey says. He walks with his hands stuffed into his jacket pockets.

"Shut up." If he can listen to my story and that's all he can come up with, who can waste time and energy talking to him? Get some layers, Joey.

"I get it," he says. We pick our way across a patch of slush that's frozen into a treacherous icy mess on the sidewalk, and I wonder what he gets. He gets that I want him to shut up?

"That stuff I said was true, about my brother." He stops walking. "People with brain injuries can be impulsive, aggressive, depressed, forgetful—" He stops, his mouth sort of hanging open, his eyes on mine for the first time more sad than angry. I nod. Yes, that stuff is true. "It doesn't add up," he says, narrowing his eyes. "He wouldn't try to kill *himself*."

I step back. No, of course not. Scott wasn't suicidal. Would he try to kill himself to avoid having a baby with me? That seems a little extreme. Like, what did he have to lose? He could have walked away at any time, and he could have gotten away with nobody ever knowing, probably, and even if his parents and everyone found out, what hardship was he going to face? His parents would love their golden boy no matter what, and besides, he was in college—it's not unheard of for college-aged boys to have sex. I shake my head.

"No," I say. "There's no way. Scott wouldn't be that irresponsible." It was far more likely that I tried to kill Scott than for him to kill himself. I dismiss the possibility.

We walk a little more quickly for the last half block to the gas station, and Joey won't let me wait outside because he says I might breathe in toxins from the gas fumes. *The baby* might breathe in toxins from the gas fumes, is what he doesn't say. Inside the station, Joey makes us linger in the candy aisle until there aren't any other customers, and then he pulls his hat down as low as it goes and tries to act nonchalant as he asks for a pack of those hipster cigarettes that are like eight bucks a pack. I hold my breath as the clerk's eyes bounce over in my direction before he reaches up for the cigarettes and asks Joey if he has any ID. "The girl, too," he says, nodding in my direction.

Joey leans in with his desperate eyes, holding up his driver's license that shows he's only sixteen years old. "Look, my brother's in intensive care right now, banged up real bad, and he might not make it. That's his girlfriend, right? We need a smoke, that's all."

I step out from behind the candy rack on the end of the aisle and the clerk takes a long look at my face, at my lacerations. He makes a show of checking Joey's ID and slides the pack across the counter with one quick motion. Joey makes them disappear like a magic trick, up his sleeve.

A block away from the station, he hands me a cigarette and a book of matches, frowning a little. "You shouldn't smoke, with the ... " He gestures vaguely with his own cigarette. "I can't believe ... " I wait, but he doesn't finish the sentence. He walks really fast.

"The clerk was staring at me like I'm some kind of freak," I say on my first exhale. I get a little dizzy, and my stomach lurches unpleasantly as the nicotine hits. Stupid baby is even ruining my one cigarette. Just let me have this one and then I'll stop. Maybe. *Stop talking to the fetus, Taylor.*

Joey makes a scary face and holds his arms out like Frankenstein's monster, staggering toward me. "Auughhh-hhrrrrauughhh," he groans.

I push him away, but he keeps coming, driving me off the edge of the sidewalk into a hedge. "Not fucking funny, asshole," I say, but I'm also sort of laughing. "I'm going to burn you with this cigarette, Joey, seriously. Get off me."

"I'm sorry," he says, his face falling back into that dark, hopeless place it's been since the rage faded. "You're going to have an awesome scar, though."

"Truth." I appreciate that Joey gets me enough to know that an awesome scar would be something I'd value, that having an interesting face might be more important to me than having a blandly beautiful face. Not that I want to carry a reminder of this on my face for the rest of my life, but it's not going to screw me up like it would some girls. I take one more dizzy puff on my cigarette before throwing it to the ground and stepping on it. Joey bends and fishes the butt out of the slush. We round the corner to the hospital.

"Ready to face the press?" He nods his head toward the hospital entrance.

"With this monstrous face?" I step through the automatic doors, the antiseptic smell of the place mingling with the smell of wet entryway carpet. We wipe our snowy sneakers and face the bank of elevators. "I'll break their cameras."

THEN

Dani and I always played this game we called Instant Vacation. The premise was pretty simple. One of us would shout out randomly, something like "Instant vacation to Washington DC!" and then we'd pretend that's where we were. Maybe I'd be like *Hey, let's climb up on the Lincoln Memorial,* and she'd be all *Look! From up here we can see into the First Lady's private chambers!* and I'd go *Let's go tell her all about our plans for world domination!* It was silly and sometimes really stupid, like one time when Dani was like *Instant vacation to Mr. Fowler's intestinal tract!* and she started talking about all the nasty stuff floating around in there and I still can't walk past him in the hall without gagging.

So Scott had been around us for a while. He knew what Dani and I were like together and he'd heard us go on lots of instant vacations. But it was our thing, between Dani and me, and Scott never participated except once. That was the thing about Scott. He didn't have to spend his time hoping and dreaming because his life was really great. He loved his family, he loved rambling around, hunting and exploring the shore of the lake along the south side of their property. There was enough money to send him to college, even without declaring a major or getting scholarships or making it onto the hockey team. He never complained.

"Instant vacation to Idaho," Dani said, tipping back her hot chocolate. Whipped cream on the tip of her nose. "I think there's a grizzly behind you."

"Retired cops," said Scott with a shrug of his shoulders. "With short tempers and big fists." He shook his head, and that's all he said. I knew he'd once spent a summer in Idaho with his great aunt and uncle while his parents were dealing with transitioning his granny into assisted living, but the few times he'd mentioned it, all he talked about was the good fishing and how much he loved the mountains.

"And potatoes," I said. I didn't know what else to say. What should I have said? There was a long silence, and Dani wiped the cream off her face and avoided both our eyes. It was awkward and drawn-out, and I was going to call out the next instant vacation, but my brain was empty of new places and all I could think about was the cops in Idaho, wondering if they had anything to do with how angry Scott had gotten at my mom and her moods.

"Instant vacation to my deer stand," Scott said at last, and his voice was low, his eyes on his hands, which were spreading butter on some kind of pastry. "It's November, and chilly enough this early in the morning to see your breath. Chilly enough to appreciate the wool jacket under your blaze orange shell."

Dani tipped her head, her hair falling in black, ironed sheets. "The sun is coming up," she said.

"The sun is coming up," Scott repeated. "It's still gray everywhere, but the sky is getting pink between the poplar trees, toward the field." He cleared his throat.

"The deer congregate in the field," I said, because I've seen them there, a herd of them. Sometimes I've watched their eyes shining in the dark when Scott pulls into the lane in his truck and turns the headlights toward the far woods.

"The first ones will walk through here before it's light enough to shoot," he said. "A doe with her two fawns, and I wouldn't shoot them anyway. I'll watch them walk beneath me. I'll see their steamy breath."

He smiled, then, and shoved the entire pastry into his gaping mouth.

NOW

Joey takes my hand when I'm finally ready to go up in the elevator. I don't know if he's still angry or what, but if it's possible to hold someone's hand defiantly, he does it. We ride to the fifth floor with his fingers gripping mine, and then the elevator swoops to a stop and he drops my hand, his face setting like sullen cement.

I breathe through the queasy moment and step over the threshold, turning right and pushing my way through the double doors. No cell phones, no noise. No idea what my boyfriend will be like when he wakes up, or what the hell his brother is thinking, holding my hand like that. It's grief, that's all. I shake my head.

The ring. The reporter. I've got to get in there, have to get into Scott's room without anyone else, but how do I get rid of his mom, of Understanding Emily? This hospital smells, and I feel like Joey and I completely reek of cigarettes, like our breath is dangerous, the air trapped in the folds of our coats. It is, actually. It's called something like third-degree smoke, and it can make people sick, babies and little kids. Once again I feel vulnerable, protective, and again I push that feeling aside.

"I've gotta..." Joey nods in the direction of the waiting room, and then he's gone. I make a beeline for Scott's room, walking silent as a nurse in my sneakers, and for three quarters of the way into the room I think I'm in luck, but then—

"Oh," says Emily, stepping out from behind Scott's IV. "I didn't hear you." She sits back down on the guest chair, the more comfortable one by his side. She holds a magazine in her lap with one hand. "The doctor gave him pinpricks in his feet," she continues, her kind eyes on my face, "and he reacted, sort of. A little movement, a little change in his facial expression."

I nod, but my face must be too blank because she rushes to explain. "He's making good progress up the Glasgow scale, Taylor. His scores are climbing in every category. This is a really good sign." She smiles a different kind of smile than usual, a smile that jumps rather than tiptoes. I smile too. A really good sign.

"Joey and I went to lunch—" The end of that sentence is complicated.

"Joey's not easy in the best of times," Emily says. "He doesn't really blame you, Taylor. None of us do. But it's hard when there are so many unanswered questions." She gets up from the chair and ushers me into it, looking deep into my eyes with that new hopeful spark. "The police came to give

Mom and Dad an overview of their investigation." Something flickers across her face. "The *accident* investigation."

We're both quiet, looking at Scott. I can't easily connect this swollen, bruised, and sleeping face to the Scott in my memory, and I can't really remember what it felt like to love him. I mean, I *care* about him, I'm not a complete horror of a person, you know. I feel kindness for him and sorrow over his pain and injuries and hope for him to recover, but I don't really feel what it means to desire him, to yearn for forever together with a kid tethered between us and that ring around my finger.

I try not to look too shifty as I peer at the floor behind Scott's bed. I can't see anything. I twist in my chair a bit to get a better view.

"Are you all right?"

My chance. Her eyes on mine are so soft, and once again I'm afraid she knows. I need her to leave the room. "Maybe..." I trail off, pressing my hand against my face as though I'm suddenly flushed, hot. "Oh, it's okay. Unless you could get me a cup of water. I'm sort of..." I leave it open-ended.

Her eyes are wide. "Oh!" She smiles and picks up a small cup off the bedside table, still wrapped in plastic. "I'll get you some from the drinking fountain in the hall. It tastes a little better."

"That's perfect, thank you so much." I'm going to have to be fast. As soon as she's past the edge of the curtain half drawn around Scott's bed, I duck down, wedging myself into the space between the wall and the machinery that checks his vitals. I see nothing, so I glance up to make sure Emily isn't coming and then I push the chair back with my ass and get all the way down on my hands and knees, pushing the cords to the side carefully, searching for a glint of gold, zirconium flakes shining against the off-white tile. Nothing.

This is so uncool. My hands skitter across the floor in all directions, reaching around the bottom of the bed. I crawl to the foot of the bed and around to the other side, hazarding a glance up at the door, hoping that Emily takes a while with the water. It's still clear, but I don't have much time so I quickly search the floor around the bottom of the curtain and climb to my feet, straightening up just as Emily enters, closely followed by a young Asian guy in a shirt and tie. The news. He carries a camera, but it's not a still camera like a person working for a newspaper would have. It's a video camera.

My phone buzzes in my pocket, and I distract myself from the intensity of Emily's kindness by pulling it out and reading the text.

I frown. The number isn't in my contacts, and the message is brief but it takes me by surprise. *Abortion is MURDER.*

"Are you all right?" Emily can clearly see I'm not, but I nod and slide my phone back into my pocket. Who would send me such a thing? I run through the list of everyone who knows, and it's a short list. Joey? Could it be him? We haven't even mentioned abortion.

Emily turns to introduce the guy behind her. "This is Tom Baker, from channel seven." He waves and gives me this little smile that manages to instantly communicate an idea of kindness, of empathy. He's also gorgeous. I look away quickly.

I stuff my hands into my hoodie, search the floor out of the corners of my eyes for the stupid ring that I don't even want, my mind fully consumed with the awful text. Can I call the number back? The thought makes my stomach lurch in a way that feels unexpected, and I give the guy a little nod, figuring there's not much more expected from the girlfriend of a boy in a coma.

"I'm doing a piece on the crash," says Tom, a thin tripod expanding like magic beneath his hands. "I mean, not all about the crash, I'm sorry if I'm being insensitive. I'm doing a series on traumatic brain injuries. So far we've talked with a couple of soldiers, and I was reading about Scott on the update site Emily set up." He's casual, non-threatening. He holds out his hand to me.

I look down. A microphone, a tiny fly to clip onto my sweatshirt, hangs between Tom's finger and thumb. I shake my head. "I don't know—"

"We don't have to show your face," he says. "Can I just...?"

My face. I allow him to attach the mic and then it all seems inevitable—the questions, interrogations. Guilt blooms in my chest, and I don't know, I don't remember. "I can't." I try to tug the mic off but my hands are heavy and numb, my heart erratic. Panic? What is this?

Tom stands beside the camera, and he has a nice smile. I focus on that, on his straight white teeth, and I breathe in, breathe out. I will not have a panic attack on television. Tom speaks, or at least his smile moves into the shape of words, but my brain snags on the sound and doesn't quite translate until a half-second later. Everything is jumbled. I look up into Tom's eyes, and he nods encouragingly at me to answer the question.

"I'm sorry, what?" I turn back to look at Scott, and Tom scoops up the camera and tripod and moves around toward the foot of the bed.

"That's great, I can get Scott in the frame and then I'll pan off of you," he says. "I was asking about how long you've known each other, maybe get you to describe Scott, the way he was before the accident, maybe what the two of you were doing on the lake, if you can talk about it." Tom gives me a small nod, lets me know he understands this is personal and a bad time and all that, but, you know, it's his job. The camera looks like something you'd see at the back of a high school play.

"We've been together for two years," I say, and then I pause. My left hand moves up on its own volition to rest on the lacerations on my face. "Scott is ... he's a wonderful guy. He loves the outdoors, especially that island on Grave Lake. In the summer he fishes from his kayak or takes me out to the island in his canoe. In the winter we take the snowmobile, and he's always careful, he always drives so safely."

"You have no memory of the crash?" asks Tom.

I shake my head. "It's all dark. I lost consciousness for a while."

"Speaking of consciousness, Scott's sister said that he's progressing as the doctors work on bringing him out of the coma." Tom leans forward. "Do you think he can feel you here? Can he hear what you say?"

"I don't know. The nurse said he can maybe smell things. I put some of his favorite candies under his nose to help him remember." I shrug and sit down on the wheeled chair, scooting Scott's bedside table out of the way so I can lean in closer to take his hand. "I've been telling him stories."

"Would you tell him one right now?"

"On camera?" My breathing has settled, my heart still fast but steady, and at least it doesn't seem like he's accusing me of anything. In fact, I might cooperate just so I can continue to look at him, to see him looking at me through a stranger's eyes. Beautiful eyes.

"Yeah, maybe you could tell a story about something hopeful, something that could help us understand what kind of person Scott is, what he hopes for and dreams about." Tom's grinning now, little scrunchy spots on the outside corners of his eyes. He's a good guy, just out of college probably. It might not hurt to tell a little story, only one. And what if I could wake him up right now, say the magic words?

THEN

(TO TOM, PLUS CAMERA)

So I'll tell about how Scott taught me how to swim. The first skill I mastered was floating. I could lie on my back in the sun and drift in the shallow water, and we both relaxed. I would float and bob in the water until I got cold and then sprawl across my Hogwarts towel on the warm sand. Scott fished the weeds along the shore for bass, which he caught and then released in a quick silver shimmer.

Casting was an act of meditation, and so was floating, and our conversation drifted in that pleasant place where both participants are truly at ease. The island was our sanctuary.

"I tried fly fishing in Idaho," he said, and I shaded my eyes, tried to read his face but it was inscrutable. "Fishing and baseball and setting up Joey with a string of grandmas to babysit him all day long so I didn't have to keep him out of the way."

I turned in a slow mermaid roll that I was beginning to perfect. "This was when you stayed with your aunt and uncle?"

"Great uncle. When my folks had to put Granny into an assisted living place because of the dementia. He was a mean one, and my great aunt only told me to get Joey out from underfoot and to keep him out until dinner time. If my folks ever knew how we were treated that summer..." Fishing line sang out as he extended his arm, a graceful zing and then a small splash as his lure hit the water.

"Did he hurt you?" I treaded water so that I could look him in the eyes. Looking for damage? Looking for danger, maybe. "Did he hurt Joey?"

Scott slowly reeled in his cast. "Fishing was the only time he wasn't angry."

NOW

My phone rumbles again in my pocket and a rush of nausea hits, my face prickling, my head spinning. "I'm sorry," I say, and I pull the mic from my collar. "I can't do this. That wasn't the right kind of story at all."

Tom takes the mic and doesn't try to stop me, though it clearly disappoints him when I ask him not to use any of that on the news. I check my phone on the bus headed home and there are two more pro-life texts, both from different numbers. I try calling the first one, my stomach uneasy as I debate what to say if someone answers. The number rings over to an automated message saying that the user is currently unavailable, and the second number does the same. The numbers don't exactly seem local. Whoever it is must be using some kind of phone number service, some kind of spammer software. Is it a real person, or a bot? I suppose it could be some kind of political activism group, but how would they know to target me? The drugstore bathroom, the shoplifted test? It's not like I purchased baby formula or prenatal vitamins or whatever. I mean, I've searched a few things on my phone about pregnancy and abortion laws and stuff, but it would be so creepy for people to be texting me based on my search history. Is that even legal? I wonder if I should take those vitamins. I shut down my phone for the rest of the night and resolve to be more careful to browse in private mode.

The next morning, I'm actually supposed to go to school. My mom clinks her spoon against the inside of her bowl, trying to get at the last of the oatmeal. "I suppose you haven't finished your homework." She sighs. "Taylor, you have to go."

I don't know what I thought was going to happen. I guess I thought that people whose boyfriends have lapsed into comas—not lapsed so much as *crashed*, I suppose—did not have to attend school. Or maybe people with lacerated faces. Or a person who is secretly pregnant and mildly amazed that no medical personnel have suspected or revealed said secret to said person's mother, for that matter.

I am not able to go to school. The thought is ludicrous. "I have a concussion." My fingers wander over the stitches on my chin. "I have memory loss."

She snorts, tossing her dish into the sink to make it clatter. "You have a C in English, for chrissakes. In *English*. The language you've been speaking since you were born."

"A C is average." I don't quibble about my speaking ability on the day I was born, though I'm tempted. I can't help it. She brings out my will to argue.

"Too bad you're not average," she says, and flicks me in the face with her wet fingers. "Now go to school."

"A half day," I plead. "The doctor would call that reasonable. I'll go to school this morning and then spend the afternoon at the hospital." Mom stops, midway through the door to the garage, her keys bouncing in her fingers. "Please."

She walks out the door with a slam, and I slump against the kitchen counter. The old garage door rattles up in its crooked tracks, and I know without waiting to listen for it that she's going to leave it for me to wrestle back down.

I pick up my phone from the edge of the table, contemplating it in my hand. I'm not sure I'm ready to face turning it back on. I need to text Dani to come get me, though, so after a moment, I power it up and brace myself for a barrage of pro-life texts. No surprise, there are three new texts, again each from a different number, and each gives me a hollow thud in my stomach. I don't even bother trying to call them back.

By the time I grab my comb and a ponytail holder, brush my teeth, and scrub the sleep out of the corners of my eyes, Dani's here. I loop my backpack over my shoulder, grab my hastily packed paper-bag lunch, and step into my boots. Dani touches the horn, twice, to let me know she's waiting, and I wrap my scarf around my mouth before opening the door. The wind is icy, and my eyelashes freeze instantly. The kid is warm inside me, I guess, but the ordinary acts of wrestling the awkward garage door and navigating the treacherous stairs down to the street feel like some kind of high-pressure test. I don't like this feeling, this lack of my usual invincible comfort. I don't like this.

"Whatcha got?" says Dani, pulling my lunch out of my hand and unrolling the top. "So awesome." She tosses her hand-sewn, quilted lunch bag into my lap. "I've had to eat that shit for two whole days, thanks to you."

Dani's mom Janie is a mommy blogger and her mom Fran is this super-vegetarian or whatever, and every day since Dani started preschool, her moms have photographed her lunches, categorized the contents, and posted recipes for all the healthy whole foods they've cleverly cut into intricate shapes and packaged in fancy, segmented, pastel containers. "Your food is good," I say, and it's true. Her lunches are filled with things like homemade frozen kale and apricot smoothies and organic tomato soup in an adorable anime thermos. I get maybe a slab of bologna on white bread with ketchup and ripple chips from a big cardboard box. Sometimes an orange or a banana, depending on when payday was.

"I can't eat it once there's a picture of it online," she says, already pulling open the foil wrapper on my Pop-Tart and stuffing part of one in her mouth. "How can I eat it when the entire Internet is watching, thinking, *This is what Dani eats for lunch*. Here's the adorable note her moms wrote to her. See how they reference that fight they all had two nights ago, which Janie completely documented online in ridiculous fucking detail so the *whole world* could chuckle at her life? Here's the whole wheat pancake sandwich, filled with the homemade raspberry jam that the whole Internet knows Dani helped Fran make last summer." She finishes wolfing down the first Pop-Tart and pulls away from the curb. "So you're alive and stuff, you asshole. I was so worried."

I can't help smiling. "I love you too." She turns away from the road long enough to make crazy eyes at me. It's a little weird about the lunch pictures, but I think Dani's moms' blog is pretty great. They've written all about the adoption, from the very beginning of the mountain of paperwork to Dani's first airplane ride home clutching Neep in her tiny brown hands to the lunch she took this morning, I suppose.

"So..." Dani trails off, but I know what she's asking, or rather, I know she's asking everything at once.

"He's the same. Everything's the same." Everything except the stupid icy sidewalk, which was trying to kill me, and my stomach, which can only tolerate pure grease. "I still can't remember anything."

She drives in silence all the way to Gordon High, then slows down but doesn't turn into the parking lot. Her old hatchback rattles past the entry and she sneaks a look at me beneath her long lashes. "Are they expecting you?" she asks, nodding toward the brick building. "Like will they call her cell?"

I relax into the passenger seat, breathing out all the anxiety I've been holding. "You have a plan?" I say. She has a plan. Dani's good at plans, and she's good at getting in trouble without getting in *trouble*.

"Momma Fran will call in for me, and she'll let us hang upstairs at the shop, do some baking, watch some movies." She steps on the gas. "I'll give you a manicure, and you can eat my froofy lunch. We need a mental health day, Taylor, that's all there is to it. We haven't even had a chance to get the hospital smell off you."

"That's a pretty good plan," I say. It's thin, but simple. I do need a mental health day, but after the way Mom argued with me, there's a pretty high chance of her checking up on my attendance. The question is, how much do I care? "My English grade isn't going to get me on any scholarship lists, though."

"Put this in your essay," says Dani, and that's that. "You're going through a bit of a rough patch." She dials her mom Fran as she drives. "You might even be a hero."

I look out the passenger window, the narrow mining company houses with their attics and dormered ceilings. It's true. But maybe I'm the villain.

THEN

It wasn't unusual for me to sneak off for an afternoon in St. Cloud, but usually Scott knew in advance that I was coming. The entire drive down there—two whole hours—my hands wouldn't stop sweating. I put the heater on full blast and alternated, one hand on the wheel and one held in front of the vent. The roads were good, the sun bright in the clear but colorless winter sky, and I squinted as I drove, wondering how the conversation would go.

"We were careful."

That's what he said, but I still can't think about the look on his face. I still don't understand the feelings I saw flitting across it. Surprise, sure, bordering on shock, but there was something of joy, too. And there's a part of me that felt so warmed by that, wanted to snuggle up in the idea of forever.

"Yeah, but you know. Still." I spread my hands like, what

else can I say? He held me, then, and he still smelled like the fitness center, where he'd been lifting. A strange glimmer of jealousy rolled over me as I felt his strong arms, but I couldn't figure out why I imagined him holding some other girl. I shrugged it off, the whole image. We had bigger things on our minds at the moment, but later, in scattered pieces, it would come back to me. What triggered the jealousy? Was there some other smell beneath the warm human scent of perspiration in the hollow of his neck, the spice of his deodorant wafting up through the embrace—was it the smell of someone else? Our visit was, by necessity, brief, and we agreed to text later, keeping "the issue" secret to be safe. I had to be back up in Sterling Creek by 2:30 at the latest. The drive back was filled with nagging thoughts about our relationship, about whether the tension in our conversations was all new or whether something had been changing before any of this ever happened.

I took a deep, steadying breath as I walked through the door of the library, inhaling the reassuring and unchanging smell of books inside the old Carnegie building. Two more deep breaths and I was sure the smell wasn't going to make me queasy. When Dani's arms enclosed me in a quiet, fierce hug, I wasn't sure if the tears welling up were from the complexities of my visit with Scott or from relief that at least this sanctuary was still sacred. I didn't know what I would do if the smell of books made me sick.

"Did he take it like a man?" It was our code for total breakdown, complete with a pint of ice cream, two spoons, and a marathon of sappy romantic comedies.

I shook my head. "He was really calm, you know. Scott-like."

Dani wrinkled her nose. "Stoic. I don't like that."

"Let's go look at weird things," I said, tugging myself out of the embrace, up the marble steps to the main level of the library. Miss Marcia smiled at us over the top of her black cheaters, looking so reassuringly like a librarian that once again a wave of relief washed over me and I had to stop to pick up a tissue from the edge of the dark wooden circulation counter that curved around toward the reference area. "Taylor. Dani, hello." She looked away respectfully, toward the stack of books she was organizing onto a shelving cart. Our feet whispered against the polished hardwood floors.

Other kids spent their time in the library working on math homework or using the library Wi-Fi to watch goofy viral videos, but we preferred the deserted microfiche room and the annals of the past that Miss Marcia so graciously allowed us to peruse according to our whims, as long as we were sure to put everything back in its place as soon as we were done. There was some really weird shit in yesterday's news, and it was almost enough to make you forget about an odd moment of jealousy or the end of your life as you had planned it to be.

NOW

Dani doesn't mess around with preliminaries. She ushers me up the stairs to the apartment above the yarn shop, a bulky cloth grocery bag looped over her arm. "I think we'll start with some cranberry white chocolate zucchini spelt muffins," she says, and she ties my apron for me because my arms are still too stiff and sore to easily reach. Although she makes fun of her mom's blog, Dani is actually the baker in her family, and many of the whole-grain contents of her faithfully photographed lunches are her own creations.

"And then you can tell me everything." She's as confident in her ability to get me to talk as she is in her ability to shout and smile and do the splits in cheerleading, or her ability to lay out all the ingredients for her muffins in five seconds flat. Mixing bowls materialize from her fingertips.

I look through the cupboards until I find the muffin pans

and the little tube of cupcake wrappers. Dani measures and stirs with a little soft hum to let me know she's waiting, listening. But giving me space. What can I say? I can tell her anything, but what do I *need* to say? The baby, the coma, the missing ring. The disturbing mystery texts that I've been receiving. The news reporter, the way Joey flipped out in the café.

"Parental notification," I say. "Forty-eight hours prior to the abortion."

"Don't worry about that. I'm on it. The hospital didn't tell her?"

I shake my head. "I...I didn't tell them. It didn't feel related to the accident."

"There are no accidents," says Dani, and then she's quiet for so long, I finish lining all the muffin cups with little pink paper wrappers while she stirs everything together in a red ceramic bowl. "Everything happens for a reason," she finally says.

I hate that, honestly. Like, I get it that people are looking for a way to make sense of bad things happening to good people and all that, but what possible reason could there be for this to happen? "I can't remember the crash, not at all. Nothing real, anyway." I watch Dani grate the zucchini into a finely shredded yellow hill. "What happened, do you think?"

"What do you mean, nothing real?"

I tell her about the image, about the red stain on the snow, about my feeling of fading into darkness. I tell her about hearing the crunch even though my ears were packed with snow from landing in that deep drift. "I think I can remember the sparkle," I say. "Snowflakes in my eyelashes. It was cold." This is new, a fresh image in my brain, and I latch onto it, persistent. The sky, a dark blue sky. It was cold. The sparkle in the light from—where was the light? A flashlight? The moon?

"Was Scott upset when you left the island? I mean, I know you were probably both upset, of course, there's a lot of stuff going on, obviously." She reaches for the rubber spatula and tips the bowl a little, scraping around the edge and drizzling the batter into the first row of muffin cups. "Did you fight?"

"I don't remember." It's a lie, and I don't know how to tell her the rest. The memory is a tightly packed kernel of unpopped corn, heating up in a pan of oil, but I'm not sure if I'd call it a fight, exactly. The ring on my finger, the absence of it now—I have to lean on the kitchen countertop and focus on my breathing. "I can't remember anything."

Dani nods, slips her hands into her oven mitts, and slides the pans onto the racks. She doesn't say anything else, but when she sets the timer, I know what she's waiting for.

"I didn't keep it from you for a reason," I say, like she already knows what I'm going to say. "It's not like I actually went through with it."

THEN

(TO DANI)

I didn't tell you. I couldn't. I didn't want to scare you. I didn't want you to see me like that, to pity me like that, or to look at me from the sides of your eyes like you were wondering, all the time, what was inside my head. What I was planning. What I'd planned.

It's like this, and I'm sorry if it's hard to just out and tell it. I didn't sleep that night, my mind a mess of soap-smells and selling kidneys to pay for abortions and a playlist of sad songs in my ears. It's not like there was a voice in my head, not something outside of myself—the playlist had run out, and I hadn't noticed the silence, and I made the decision to jump. It felt very sensible, and I saw what would happen with the certainty of something that had already occurred. I would jump into a frozen mine pit, break my neck, and it would be over. I couldn't see any way past this vision, somehow.

I walked to the cliff, which was a lot farther than I had bargained on, plus I was surprised by how long it took for the sun to come up. My feet were on fire with the cold by the time I got there, and it was still pitch black. I almost threw myself over the edge just to stop feeling cold, but I wanted to notice the pink light of sunrise. I wanted to see everything.

This idea wasn't entirely new, you know. There was always my fascination with the story of Petra Jarvi—the girl whose daddy allegedly pushed her over the edge and then hanged himself in the shack on the ridge. Petra Jarvi, who would pull me to the bottom of the pit by one ankle and never let go. I always wondered about the girl, though. Was she alive when she fell? Was she really pushed, or did she jump?

It wasn't going to work. My whole life was broken. My mom was going to find out, and I was going to be reduced to a problem like some kind of trash can that needed to be emptied. Dirt to wash out. These thoughts were like solid iron, heavy—dragging me toward the edge of the cliff. I leaned. I inhaled and closed my eyes.

I don't know how close I got to the edge. My memory narrows down to a black pencil point of a moment, and I know that if I remember the lip of that cliff beneath my feet—if I see how close I was to being that girl—I'd lose my mind. It was too close.

And then I stepped back. I was dizzy and cold and pregnant, but when it got right down to it, I saved myself instead of flinging myself into oblivion. So I figure I must want to live, even if it didn't feel like it right then.

NOW

The oven door bangs shut. "You seriously thought you couldn't tell me that?" says Dani. She holds her two oven-mitted hands out, one painted with sunflowers and the other with rainbow-striped goldfish.

"You. Giant. Idiot." The words equal a whack of sunflowers followed by two whacks of rainbow fish. "Of all the people in the world?" She throws the mitts to the kitchen floor and puts her arms in my face. I turn away.

"Look at them, Taylor. Look, or I'll let the muffins burn." Again, she pushes her arms to me, her wrists extended.

"You wouldn't do that," I say, but I look, and like always, my eyes fill up with sorrow to see her scars. I cover them with my hands. "I wasn't going to do it, but now you'll think I did it for sure. That I crashed the snowmobile to, like, kill myself."

Dani crouches to pick up the oven mitts. She pulls the

muffins out, and the room fills with the warm smell of fresh baking. "Well, did you? I wouldn't judge." The pans clatter against the stove top, and the sound comforts me.

"I don't know," I say. "I remember snowflakes on my eyelashes, blue sky, and a kind of light. Or blood on white snow. Or nothing."

She nods and leaves the oven propped open so the heat shimmers up behind her. "Well, I'm glad you stepped back."

THEN

(TO DANI)

I walked away from the pit, my thoughts still dark and too sharp to hold on to, and I couldn't be alone with myself anymore, so I called Scott. And I needed him to be strong. I needed him to be someone who wouldn't judge me. Like he could have said, "Hey, Taylor, thank you for not jumping off a cliff because, you know, I love you," or even, "Whoa, your feet must be freezing." Instead, he freaked out, big-time angry, and angry wasn't at all what I needed.

So the thing is, I'm exceptionally good at getting yelled at. You would know that, but I guess he forgot. I kept putting one foot into the snow and then the next, the whole time he went on about how I didn't have the right to make that kind of decision for the baby. For his baby. After about a block and a half of this I realized that I could hang up my phone instead of listen, so I did, and he called back immediately. I didn't answer. He called back five more times, and on the fifth time I picked up the phone and was like, "What." No expression, just what.

"I'm sorry," he kept saying. "That was stupid, Taylor. I was caught off guard. I'm worried about you." He told me to hang in there until Saturday evening, after his shift at the oil change place—you know, he worked there on the weekends he was home. He said I should dress warm. He said he would have a surprise.

And I couldn't get over it. I stewed over his reaction all week, my brain unable to focus on anything. Saturday night, I waited by the window, and I tried to forgive him, but I was about to break up with him.

NOW

My mom starts calling after lunch, irate. I don't answer, but she fills my voicemail with vitriol and then starts in on the texting, so I have to tell her where I am just to shut her up. Dani says to turn off the phone, but it would be just like my mom to call the police and say that I'm suffering from a head injury and possibly deranged or something, get them to hunt me down like a wild animal lurking amid the knitting needles, desperate.

I can't pass the row of baskets by the till without running my fingers over the balls of wool huddled together like sleeping kittens inside each one, without pinching the thick felt on Fran's felting station. Everything in Dani's mom Fran's world has a soft, steady order to it. I have to turn myself to steel to walk through the bright yellow wooden door and into the world of my mother, who waits in the car. Her eyes drill through the windshield at me.

"I've got my phone," says Dani, from behind me, and she tugs on my hood twice.

"I'll be all right," I say. The passenger door is so heavy. I drag myself into the car, which is filled with the smell of my mother's perfume—a bright, round shiny thing like a new coin.

"She won't stop texting me," says my mom, and her tone is so light, it's a complete mismatch with her intense gaze and her perfume and her voicemail.

"I—" have no idea what she's talking about.

"Dani. Telling me I need to listen, I need to be fair to you, I need to give you a chance to talk." She looks down at her phone as she speaks, her eyes seeking out the bifocals in her lenses. "She's quite persuasive."

"I didn't know—"

"I know." She swipes the phone screen to black and drops it into the console, shifting the car into drive. "The school nurse called me, I called you, I was a jerk on your voicemail." She sighs and checks her mirror, then pulls away from the curb. "I was scared, Taylor. Okay? I was scared for you. So I called the psychologist from the hospital."

"The lady I already talked to?"

"Celeste somebody." Mom taps her nails against the wheel. "Post-trauma counseling or whatever. She's fitting you in now, on an emergency basis, based on the fact that you completely disappeared from school and nobody could find you and we were like five minutes from calling out an Amber Alert."

"Yeah?" I'm trying to figure out how I feel about the

therapy thing. I don't believe her about the Amber Alert, but it was probably still a good idea I didn't turn off my phone.

"So I called the nurse back and told her I'd completely forgotten about your therapy appointment and you'd be back in school tomorrow." She puts on her blinker and turns onto the street that crosses over the Sterling Creek to the hospital side of town, where a kind woman named Celeste waits in her office to help me find my way.

THEN

I talked a lot, when Scott and I were together. He was kind of quiet, and when I'm around quiet people, if they're not going to talk, I will. Sometimes I'd get on a roll, going on about something that was really interesting to me, and Scott would put both of his hands on my shoulders and stare me into silence with this funny grin on his face. Then he'd be like "I love you, Taylor," and it was all perfect, like the earth rotated only for our sakes. I know he really liked what I had to say, but I also know it wasn't always the case that my opinions and thoughts were so charming to him that he just had to stop me and kiss me. There were times when he was tolerant of my talking, as long as I would kiss him.

I talked my way through that entire visit to the island, talked my way through any chances he might have taken to spring his surprise. I talked about everything but what

I wanted to say to him, that we needed to break up, that I needed some space, that I had some thinking to do. All those things were too difficult, and I wondered if he would stop and listen to me. He made a fire and wrapped a wool blanket around me, and I prattled on about anything and everything besides babies and drop-outs and welfare moms and break-ups. I talked even when he did the thing with his hands on my shoulders and his smile; I kept my eyes averted.

"Taylor, listen to me for a second. Listen." He was still smiling but he was getting irritated. I wouldn't even let him apologize the right way, wouldn't let him get around to his surprise. I was terrified. I *knew* him. I knew Scott, knew his steadiness. I couldn't have even had said, if you'd asked me right then, why I didn't want to give Scott the satisfaction of *a moment*, but I was scared, and on some level I knew he was going to do the right thing, and by that I mean the exact opposite of the right thing.

He caught me. It's not like I could say no. He got on one knee and everything, and I just wanted him to stand up. He was embarrassing me, and I wanted to run. I was filled with the urge to escape, to turn my back and walk out on this particular life, but of course I was surrounded, trapped on this island with everything so inevitable in the way I just *hate*—and at the same time everything that is so tempting and beautiful. Happily ever after.

NOW

I keep checking myself, this little mental status update where I try to figure out if I feel pregnant. The therapist's name is Celeste, and I've already spent a considerable amount of time thinking about how absurd that name is for this heavy-set woman with her lipstick settling into the small, papery crinkles around her mouth.

"I still don't remember anything," I say when she ushers me into her office—a real, walls-all-the-way-to-the-ceiling kind of office with a closing door—in the central wing of the brain trauma unit. Mom drops me off and goes back to work helping other people's kids.

"Oh, it's early," says Celeste, settling herself into one chair. The office is small, and there's no desk at all, though there are lots of dark wooden storage compartments with orange bins. Three chairs are arranged near a rug and an end table, like it's someone's living room, and as I perch on the edge of the same chair I sat on that first time, I wonder what this is all about. Is she going to try to talk to me about the crash, or is this going to be about skipping school today? No matter what, I can't tell her what I told Dani, or she'll put me in the ward for suicidal girls or whatever. It's one floor down from here; it would be easy to push me into a wheelchair and then whoosh, everyone in my entire life believes that I'm the girl who tried to kill herself on a snowmobile and ruined her boyfriend's life.

"You weren't ready for school today," says Celeste, interrupting my thoughts. She smiles, and I'm taken aback. She's sincere, like this deep kind of real, and I can see it there right in her eyes. I could tell her anything. "I'm glad you answered your mom's messages so we knew you were safe."

"I was baking muffins with my best friend. We just needed a day, you know?"

She knows, actually. She sees this kind of thing all the time. Well, not exactly this kind of thing. I don't know. I think I might trust her. She doesn't respond, but she waits, and I know I'm going to talk again; it's just a matter of how long I can hold out. If I want to hold out. Somewhere in the back of my head there's a little salty pool, and if I let the tears spring forth, I'm not sure if there'll be a bottom. I focus on school, on this morning. Nothing else.

Celeste doesn't push. She pulls one of the orange bins down off the wall and takes out a glue gun and a big bag of sparkly things. She plugs it in and spills the plastic beads and things into a plastic tray. Then she takes out a little plastic jar, like maybe it used to have lotion or bath beads in it but it's all spray-painted glossy white, and the lid has a slot cut into it, like a piggy bank. She busies herself with other little tasks, like she's forgotten that it's my therapy time and not arts and crafts hour. She's humming softly, kind of flat actually, and I wish she would stop. But she keeps sorting through the bead tray, laying out the ones she likes on the table near the jar.

"Are you making some kind of can for donations?"

She smiles and shakes her head. "This job doesn't pay much, but things aren't that bad." She drops a couple of beads inside the jar, puts the lid back on, and gives it some good shakes. "This is for you, silly. It's for your memory collection. So you can write about what you remember." She hands me a handful of half-sheets of paper, each with some lines and some white space. "You can write on these by hand, or you can print out the memories you've written on your phone," she says.

"Do you read them?" Some of the memories I've written already are not things I'd want her to see, I don't think.

She smiles and shakes her head again. "Only if you share them with me," she says, and I completely believe her. "Here you go. The glue is hot."

THEN

(MEMORY JAR)

He got down on one knee. It was ridiculous. I wouldn't let him speak until he stood up, and even then I pointed at his knee and said, "You're getting wet."

He looked down. The snow was sloppy, wet from the heat of the fire, and it had already soaked through the first layer of his snow pants, maybe all the way through. "You'll get cold," I said.

I wanted to step away from him. I wanted to *run* away from him, but I'd have settled for turning away from his stare. I would step toward the fire, pretending I was cold, but Scott had me trapped, his eyes so intense, deep sapphires in the glow of the flames. The sky was still light, a kind of smear of gray behind him, and I didn't want this to happen. I didn't want any of this to happen.

"Taylor. Please. We can make this work."

I opened my mouth, but he held up a hand and the words tumbled out. "Just marry me, okay?" He fumbled at a small box with his gloves on for a moment and then gave up and pulled the gloves off with his teeth. "M'seriousmmm," he said through the gloves, and then he tipped the little box over into my hand so the ring fell out onto the palm of my red mitten.

Did any person ever in the history of anything dream of this moment? Is this anyone's dream come true? To have another person gaze into your eyes with something like love, perhaps, but also like panic—to have that someone stick a glove into their mouth and mumble out the words, "Just marry me, okay?" There are so many awful things in the world that happen, and yes, I knew that nobody dreams of those either. People getting shot up in the streets by gangs or backing over their own children in their own SUVs or dying in wars or whatever else, and yeah, those things are stupid and I hated them too, but that moment, in the snow, on the island, with that ridiculous ring lying on the palm of my mitten—was that what my life was going to be? Every single second I was learning the magnitude of my one mistake and trying to puzzle out the future of two million possibilities.

My mom was married once. That was fun. Wait, I don't even know if that was sarcasm or not because, see, it *was* fun, and I liked Grady. That was his name, but I was only seven and a half so I called him Gravy because it made me giggle and he didn't mind. I got to wear a red satin dress with a big heart on the back because they got married on Valentine's Day. He was good to my mom, but he was lazy, and he smoked a little too much dope, and I can remember her nagging him about his lack of *ambition*, even though I had only a hazy idea what that meant at the time. She pushed him away, but while she was busy with that she was extra sweet and gentle with me, the wary kid. I didn't want this baby to have to grow up wary like that, and what if he did? Scott would never leave me, but what if I deserved to be left? There were so many stupid what ifs in this whole stupid situation.

I can't marry you, Scott. If I had found the courage to say those words, would anything be different? Would we have left the island earlier, while there was still light in the sky? Would we have avoided the ice ridge? Would any of this be real?

Sometimes I do this thing where I have a conversation over and over in my head until it's right. Until it's fixed, and I no longer stood there dumbfounded with a ring in my hand. A ring that didn't feel like an answer.

I put the stupid ring on my finger to keep it safe. It didn't feel like I was saying yes.

NOW

There's a name for this stage, a new name, and it involves Scott moving away when they pinch his fingernails and making noises that may or may not be words. They're waiting for him to open his eyes when people talk to him, so of course everyone's in there talking to him non-stop. I still don't see the ring anywhere, though I keep my eyes skimming around the room as I walk in, wondering as I do what exactly I should do if I see it lying somewhere. Do I claim it?

Celeste walks me all the way to Scott's room after my session, says I should take the memory jar with me. She gives me a stack of slips to fill out. The two beads she threw in originally are still there, rolling around, their clunking somewhat softened by the memories I've already put in: the ones from my phone that Celeste helped me print, plus a few more I scribble out on paper. I don't write about me bleeding on the snow and Scott holding my hand as I died because objectively, that memory is not real, no matter how it feels. Grappling with reality is all I do right now. It can't be healthy.

"Taylor! We were just talking about you!" Emily folds me into a hug and stands beside me, beaming. The late afternoon sun shines in the window behind Scott's father, who nods at me without quite looking at me, and it lights up his mom's face as she turns to greet me. She holds her arms out and I lean in for a hug, even though she never used to hug me. She smells like hospital coffee and she feels so tiny and birdlike and fragile. Even though she never blames me, her embrace fills me with guilt.

"Any change?" I fold my arms across the front of my body, feeling all their eyes on me. I look at Scott, who looks mostly like he did yesterday, with slight changes to the coloration of his bruises. Well, not entirely like before. There's something a little different about the way his body rests in the bed, something more relaxed—less couch-cushiony.

"He opened his eyes and tried to talk," says his mother, with a quick nod, but she slips into a small smile. "Nothing we could understand, and not really in response to anything we did, but it's progress."

It's progress. Toward a minimally conscious state, which is better than a persistent vegetative state. My head swims with states.

This is so crazy. We're all gathered around his bed marveling over his ability to move his fingers and make an unintelligible sound. What's going on in his *head* is what I want to know. How much of Scott is inside that skull now? Will he still remember me? Will he still love me?

"Hey, Taylor. Glad you showed up." I look up, toward the door, and there's Joey, a weird grin on his face. "I forgot to give you this yesterday." His hand is in the pocket of his jeans, digging for something small, and I know he's going to do it—he's going to pull out that engagement ring right in front of his mom and dad, so I'll be trapped all over again. Who knows, maybe he's going to tell them all about the baby thing too.

"It's okay, I don't need it right now." I hold up my hand to stop him, but it's too late; Joey's already reaching toward me. "No! It's—"

It's ten bucks. He shakes the crumpled bill in my face a couple times until I take it, holding it between my thumb and index finger, puzzled. "What's this?"

"For lunch, obviously." He rakes his fingers through his hair and then brushes it down in front of his eyes, turning away toward the window. "I'm the one who asked if you wanted to go, and then you end up buying my food. Didn't want you to think I planned it that way."

I can't keep from smiling, relief sweeping over me, and a little shame for thinking he'd betray my confidence like that. But after all, as recently as a day ago he was basically accusing me of murdering his brother. Attempting to murder.

"So." Joey speaks into the room, which has fallen into that tired hush of people who've been spending a lot of time talking to each other in waiting rooms. "You guys could go take a walk or something, and Taylor and I could talk to Scott a little bit."

It's the kind of thing I would never say to them, but the only way I'll ever get a chance to be alone with Scott again.

His parents sort of nod their heads and murmur their goodbyes and slip out of the room. Scott's dad rubs his mom's back as they walk toward the elevators, and it's the sweetest thing. It's the kind of thing Scott would have done for me. Caring. Selfless. This whole family is pretty much intolerably good. Even Joey, who walks his sister down the hall and gives me a moment alone with his brother.

THEN

(TO SCOTT)

I put my mitten back on, and the damage was done—the ring was on my finger. I don't mean that, Scott. I don't mean that about the damage. I didn't know what to do, okay? How can anyone expect me to know what to say about marriage when I'm barely seventeen years old? Did you even know what I wanted out of life? Did you know what my dreams were? Did you know what you were asking of me?

I remember the mitten, I remember you holding me and me letting you, and you were warm and it was getting dark and then it was really dark, and there was no moon and the snow was freezing my feet and we sat on that chair so I could put my feet up to the fire as it died, but I wanted to go home.

I wanted to be alone, but not this alone, okay? It's the

way I am; I need time to process things, and there was a lot to process. I asked you to bring me home and you said you would. I don't remember.

I can't remember.

Or maybe I won't remember.

NOW

Joey comes back into the room, sliding into his dad's seat by Scott's left hand. He says hello, chats his brother up like it's a normal day. I lean back into the chair on the opposite side of the bed, but I'm watching Joey, not Scott.

"You're good at that," I say after a while. "You're good at talking to him so naturally." He's calling his brother back, over whatever time and space is squished up in between the impact of that ice and a few ounces of gray matter. "You're talking to him like he's the same."

Joey smiles. "I read this thing once about the guy who did the voice for Bugs Bunny, you know? 'What's up, Doc?'" Joey holds an imaginary carrot in his hand and makes this face that's so hilariously similar to Bugs Bunny in that scene that I burst out laughing. "No, seriously," he says. "The dude got into a car crash or something, and they couldn't get him out of a coma or whatever until some doctor called him Bugs or something, and then the dude sat right up and started living again, his normal self."

We fall silent at that and turn our expectant attention to Scott, who does not sit right up and start living again, his normal self. There's a long moment of quiet, and then Joey does the Bugs Bunny thing and we both burst out laughing. I look around and I realize, *this* is a memory I want to put in my memory jar.

"I have a story for you," says Joey after a while. "For Scott, I mean."

THEN

(JOEY)

That summer we were in Idaho, when Scott was nine and I was six, we played baseball every day all summer long at the school ball fields, up the hill and across from the old cattle-feed warehouse. Scott and his friends, they never let me play unless I did what they said. Monkey Boy, they called me, and they would make me climb to the top of the dugout, or up to the top of the chain-link fence behind home plate. They used to make me carry all their bats, so I put them in my metal wagon and dragged them up the alley and across Fourth Avenue. All the older ladies doing their gardening would hear those rattling bats and come out to say hello.

Sometimes they would give me coins that I could take down to the gas station on the corner of the alley and buy enough candy to give me a belly ache. This was pure heaven for a country kid who'd never had access to a corner store before, and who was under the supervision of a great aunt who had no desire to care for children. "Home by dark, and nothing broken," was her daily command. My great uncle occasionally took us fishing, but mostly he spent his days stomping around that old stale-smelling bedroom and growling at anyone who got in his way.

The older boys got mad that I was holding up their game talking with the neighbors, so they started hauling their own bats, but I didn't care. I decided to fill my wagon with something else. Something I could sell.

I thought about taking garden tools and offering my services as a weed-puller, but that sounded like a lot of work, and also, all these old ladies really seemed to love scooting around on those little rolling garden benches, digging in the dirt with their big hats on. I thought about what old ladies might want to buy. I thought about my granny, who liked reading books about the covered wagon days and dusting the mantel and cooking weird-smelling versions of the things my mom told her I liked, and then I remembered she was losing her little house, that my parents were taking her to that place that smelled kind of like pee. I missed her terribly. My great aunt was no substitute, and my great uncle was just plain mean.

Some of the ladies talked to me like I was a grown-up, using big words and asking what I was thinking about. One of the women always sang to me, religious songs. Her voice was high and thin and warbly, like a fragile bird, and I didn't like to leave her yard because she kept on singing while she waved goodbye. Scott and his friends thought I was stupid. They couldn't imagine talking to a bunch of old people. As nice as he always was to everyone else, Scott was the first one to say, "Hey, Monkey Boy, smells like you forgot to change your Depends," which started everyone saying that.

But one morning it rained, hard and windy, with a dangerous storm predicted, and there was no baseball, no prowling the town for us. My brother and I were fighting in the living room, trying to wrestle each other into the scratchy orange rug. Scott pushed my face into the floor, scrubbing my cheekbone hard enough against the rug to give me a big red mark, and when I jumped up and ran to show Aunt Thea, she was completely exasperated. She looked out at the rain falling from the sky in sheets, and I know she was considering sending us out in it anyway.

"I'd like you boys to make a house-warming card for Grandma Wendy," she said, and she got a sad plastic bag of markers out of her kitchen junk drawer and a packet of construction paper. As I sat there scribbling slap-dash, dry-markered flowers, an idea occurred to me that would, for the first time in my life, give me the upper hand over my big brother. I sort of thought it would be the kind of thing that would make Scott start taking me seriously, as a person.

As soon as the sun came out again, I carefully dried out my red wagon and filled it with Auntie's markers, the packet of paper, a pair of scissors from the kitchen drawer, and a set of pinking shears I stole out of her sewing basket. As usual, the ladies came flocking to meet me, many of them with extra smiles since they hadn't seen me the day before. They were all charmed by my entrepreneurial spirit. I told them they could order a greeting card, tell me what they wanted me to write and what kind of design they would like (though I strongly suggested motorcycles, dragons, or ninjas, if the customer wasn't interested in a quick squiggle of flowers, which was my specialty), and I would create the card *right while they waited,* which I said every time like it was some kind of remarkable great deal.

I gave Scott a chance to weigh in on this, to get in on the deal. I offered to let him come along. I asked him for his financial advice, even, wondering how much I should charge for each card. He laughed at me, rolled his eyes in a way he had just mastered that summer. "Nobody is going to buy your ugly cards," he told me, and for the next two weeks, that was the phrase I made sure he heard repeated most often.

Because I was rolling in the big bucks with this venture. The ladies *loved* ordering cards, and they *loved* coming up with new things for me to draw and helping me write things on the cards. Some even sat with me and came up with a few lines of poetry, and one lady taught me how to draw a curling vine across the edges of the cards with little rose buds every few inches. Maybe because of Scott's statement, I never did come up with a price for the cards. I just asked for a donation, and that was the best business strategy ever. Those women were dying to give me the coins they'd gathered in their purses, or even sharply creased dollar bills that smelled like baby powder.

They added art supplies to my wagon—tubes of glitter glue or sticker sheets, ribbon scraps, and little plastic capsules full of sequins. I sat on their gardening carts and colored and glued, and then I took my wagon down to the store, loaded it with candy, and resold the candy to the guys at the baseball fields for a small delivery fee, which they grumbled about but paid anyway, unable to resist the sight of my tempting merchandise. By the end of that summer, I had a crew of regular customers who ordered their candy the day before.

The part Scott will probably remember, though, is when he tried to get in on the profits by pushing me to the ground and punching me. I can still remember the look on his face when my aunt raised her voice, pulling him off of me with a stern frown. "You can't go punching people just because they do something better than you," she said.

NOW

We both look at Scott now, quiet and still, and the note of victory in Joey's story falls a bit flat. "It didn't work," says Joey, and he looks as heavy as I've ever felt.

"You don't know that," I say. "On some level, he's hearing every word."

He nods, slowly. "I guess I wasn't talking about right now," he says. "I was thinking that it didn't work, getting Scott to take me seriously as a person."

I want to argue, to reassure, but I don't have anything. I don't even have a sibling to know what it's like. "Let's keep trying," I say, and I take a peanut butter cup out of my backpack. "It was last Halloween."

THEN

(TO JOEY, FOR SCOTT)

We were too old for trick-or-treating, obviously, but we wanted to dress up and we wanted to eat candy, and none of us had our own place to hold a party, so we ended up driving around in Scott's truck. Looking for trouble, I guess, but nothing big. A little mischief at most. It was me, Scott, Dani, and her artist friend Melinda, I think, in the front seat. We were all squished into two bucket seats, basically. I was straddling the gear shifter and pretending to get mad at Scott when he took advantage of that. Or tried to, since my mummy costume wasn't exactly easy to take advantage of.

"Every girl dresses slutty on Halloween, but you're all wrapped up in bloody gauze like a wisdom tooth extraction," he said.

"It's fucking cold," I said. For the rest of the night, when-ever someone asked about my costume, I said I was dressed up as a wisdom tooth extraction. It was much more fun than a mummy. Halfway through the night, we even stopped and picked up a sale-price doctor's costume for Scott, so he could be the dentist, and he gave up his giant werewolf head to his buddy Cody, who was stuffed into the tiny backseat of the truck with this girl Maren. He was dressed like a hockey player, which was lame because he played hockey in high school just like Scott. Werewolf hockey player was much better. Maren wore a gigantic referee shirt and didn't say much, though she took some really cool pictures of us with an old Polaroid.

We did all the usual things—coffee and creamer-flipping at the Village Inn, walking around downtown halfheartedly trying to get served in a couple of the less-attentive bars, succeeding in one, driving over to the fast food taco place and eating more than we should have, and finally it was late enough and dark enough and creepy enough for us to sneak into the graveyard with the Ouija board. This wasn't the new cemetery near the highway and the mall, the one with lighted statues and those big mausoleum things that some lumber baron bought back in the day and they moved them and all the dead bodies over when they dug out the mine pits under-neath that edge of the town. This was the graveyard, the one between the elementary school and the old water tower.

The sky was overcast, even though there was a bright moon shining out every so often. It was cold, enough to see your breath. We could stay warm enough if we huddled together, and my bandages made nice layers.

Under a shifty dark sky, we shushed our way through the overgrown path and over the wrought iron gate. Scott and Cody positioned themselves on either side of the gate and helped the girls over. We stumbled and giggled, trying to stay quiet and mostly failing. There was a path around the edge of the graves, but it was overgrown, and we tripped in the dark over patches of weeds and brambles.

Scott kept eating these peanut butter cups, the little ones, popping them in his mouth one after another, and I was like following his peanut buttery trail through the dark, wondering about ghosts. Dani read us this poem by Edgar Allan Poe, about some dead lost girl, and it gave me these little tingles up and down the back of my neck. As always, I kept on thinking about Petra Jarvi, tugging on my feet off the end of the dock, and then even my mummy layers couldn't keep me from shivering violently.

"Ask it when I'm going to die," Scott said. He was cocky, or filled with bravado, anyway. The plastic triangle on the Ouija board settled beneath our fingertips, all of us with two fingers touching. It seemed to vibrate, like the board was a liquid and it was a windblown leaf, and then it clattered across the board in a haphazard circle.

"It's really moving," said Dani, crowding her shoulder into mine. "Seriously, who's pushing it?"

But it didn't feel like anyone was pushing it. The planchette flew across the board, our fingertips sliding at times trying to keep up. It swung around and around, erratic and fast. A giggle rose up in my throat, and my hands were like ice. I was freezing.

"I changed my mind," said Scott, laughing, but the thing moved swiftly to NO.

"No?" It was Dani, her face absolutely surreal in her zombie prom queen makeup. Her tiara sat crookedly over a very realistic head wound. "What do you mean, no?" She looked at Scott, and the plastic triangle flew over the board, whipping from letter to letter. As it flew by each letter, the planchette seemed to stop—decisively, quickly—how could one of us be pushing it? It made an urgent circle and then flew on to the next letter. DREAMNODEAD.

It was done. Gone. The plastic triangle sat flat and still against the board. "You have to say goodbye," said Dani. "You have to release the spirit."

"I think the spirit's gone," muttered Maren, and she took her fingers off the planchette so she could operate her camera. We dragged the spirit across the words GOOD-BYE anyway, just to be safe.

Scott chuckled. "Dream no dead," he said. "Dream. No. Dead."

"Dude, I think it means you're a zombie," said Cody.

I was a little creeped out, but Scott smiled and pushed Cody's arm. "Everybody's a zombie tonight, buddy," he said, and then he pretended to bite Cody's face off. "Braaaaiiiiins."

Dani took my hand, though, and she leaned in close. "Dream no dead?" she whispered. "What the fuck does that mean?"

NOW

Joey and I exchange a wide-eyed look. "Dream no dead?" We both look at Scott's prone form and then back at each other.

"That's creepy," he says, his hands curling into fists. "I don't like that shit at all."

"I didn't realize until..."

"Yeah." He looks away, breaking eye contact. "I'm sorry. I still don't know how to feel if I don't feel angry. I'm losing my mind."

I wave it away. "Look at him." I reach across Scott to show my phone to Joey. "He had some kind of *tool* in his truck, like a real creepy dentist." In the picture, Scott is making evil butcher dentist faces and pretending to dig in my mouth with these metal clamp things. By this time we had splattered fake blood all over his scrubs. It was pretty gruesome.

Joey has an easy laugh, for once. "The clamps," he says and

laughs even harder, but he won't tell any more, even after I protest that I've been sitting here spilling my guts and he can't even tell me the only thing that's made him relax in three days? He refuses, grinning the whole time though, like a person whose life might go on even if his brother is in a minimally-persistent/partially-vegetative/slightly-conscious/barely-even-there kind of way. Even if his brother's girlfriend is horrible.

"Whatever," I say. "It's probably disgusting."

"It probably is." He doesn't say anything more, but he fiddles with the brim of his hat again, pulling it lower and then lifting it off, over and over. He still smiles, his face relaxed in a way I'm not sure I've ever seen it, even before the crash. And I'm staring at him like a creeper.

We're quiet, and the room is quiet, and I clear my throat because the air is dry.

"Ahem." The sound comes from the bed.

Joey and I look at each other, then back at Scott. He's not moving, not looking any different at all. Was it a coincidence? Did he and I clear our throats coincidentally at the same time? Joey repeats the same noise, twice. "Ahem, ahem."

There's a long pause, and nothing. Joey's shoulders sink down in a way that lets me know he was holding his breath, and mine probably do too. He reaches into his jacket pocket then and pulls something out, holding it in his hand. "Found this," he says, and he tosses me this little cellophane packet. I catch it. Sealed in the cellophane from Joey's cigarette pack is my engagement ring. "Didn't want it to get dirty," he says. The ring looks like drugs, something illicit nestled in a pillow of plastic.

"Thanks." I put my hand into my hoodie pocket, cradling the ring, and there's this look—I can't explain it—between me and Joey. It's like, I want to say it's like we *understand* each other, but that's not exactly it. It's like we're acknowledging each other's enigmas and coming to the decision that we can like each other anyway. Then there's another noise from the bed.

"Ahem ahem."

THEN

(MEMORY JAR)

Dream No Dead. Do I dare hope for him to wake up, miraculous, and start telling us all about his trip to Oz? I remember the time when we fell asleep together, a rare overnight in Scott's dorm room when his roommate was out of town and Dani could cover for me with my mom.

Scott woke up first, and he was looking at me, propped up on his elbow, when I opened my eyes. There was a soft look about his mouth. "I dreamed about you," he said, and he smiled.

I smiled back. "Was I crushed by an avalanche or charged by a runaway bull or something?" Most of the dreams I can remember involve things like that happening to me.

His eyebrows bobbed in amusement. "Not exactly," he

said. "But you did turn into a bird for a minute, I think. Or else you were just covered in feathers, I don't know." He shook his head. "I never saw you fly."

I wonder if he wakes, if he'll have memories of the time he's been sleeping. I wonder if he'll remember the stories.

NOW

Joey rings for the nurse and describes the throat clearing. She listens without changing her expression and promises to update Scott's doctor. Scott's mom comes back and sits beside him, and she makes a number of noises in the hope that he'll repeat them. We all hang around and listen for a long time, but either the whole thing was a complete coincidence or it was an isolated incident, because nothing seems to be happening now.

I check my phone and see that it's almost time, and my mom is going to be here soon to pick me up. My stomach is queasy at the uncertainty of everything, especially everything involving my mother. If things were always like this afternoon, I could tell her what was happening. I'd tell her and we'd figure it out together. Would she sign an agreement to let me abort?

"It's progress," says Emily, with another embrace. So many people hugging me who never did before. And me, accepting the hugs. Leaning into them, even. "What's in your little container?" She points to the memory jar.

I hold it close to my chest. "It's for my therapist. I'm writing down the memories I have of Scott."

Her whole face lights up—she believes I'm doing this *for* Scott."That's a wonderful idea, Taylor. Maybe we should all be doing that." She pulls me close one more time, presses her mouth up close to my ear, and whisper-sobs, "I truly believe he's going to pull out of this."

I nod, my eyes glazed over with tears, and squeeze her back. I don't even know what I'm feeling, but it might be helplessness. It might be hope. In my pocket there is a little crinkle of cellophane as she hugs me tight.

"You want me to walk down with you?" says Joey, shrugging like he doesn't care.

"Cool," I say, and I shrug too. We're cool as anything. "Let's take the stairs instead of the elevators."

Joey descends with both hands in his pockets, shoulders hunched. "Do you think he's going to wake up?" His voice echoes in the stairwell.

I like the spiraling of staircases, and I lean on the center rail a little, even though there's this strange undercurrent of thinking about germs, about vulnerability. "I don't know, maybe." The yellow light makes everything look sick and sallow. "I want to know what his brain is going to be like. What *he's* going to be like."

Joey nods, takes a hand out of his coat pocket to hold open the door to the parking garage. "I do and I don't," he says.

I walk through the door, into the chill of the evening.

No sign yet of my mom on the street outside, and the wind when we step out past the entryway of the garage is bitter cold. I pull the scarf up around my throat and bury my face in it. "This is ridiculous."

Joey pulls me back into the stairway before I realize what he's doing, and for an awkward second we bump into each other and his arm is wrapped weirdly around me and everything is all strange and close, and then we fall apart from each other and look away. "I'll wait for her out there, and you can stay warm," he says. "No sense both of us freezing our asses off."

"Thanks," I say, but he hesitates, and I don't want him to leave.

THEN

(TO JOEY)

I remember the smell. That day I first told him, when he hugged me, I remember what it was that made me uneasy. It wasn't perfume; that would have been too easy, too expected. He was working out, sweaty. I smelled him, but there was something else, there must have been. Deodorant, maybe? Could he have borrowed someone else's deodorant? Could someone else have been in his arms, someone else who was working out? Someone who smelled like soap.

We knew it was going to be difficult, with him at college and me in high school. "It's the way it goes," I told him. "The girl back home? You think that ever actually works?" The whole long-distance relationship thing didn't seem all that likely to make it, honestly.

Scott swore that I was the one for him, and I think he actually believed it, which was fine with me. I didn't worry about him cheating on me, I don't know why. I suppose you'll jump to the conclusion that I didn't care, but that's not true. I cared, but I was also busy living, you know? I had Dani and high school, and I still got to see him every other weekend or so when he came up, even though my mom wouldn't let me go down to St. Cloud to see him. That pissed me off, the way she wouldn't even listen, absolutely refused to let me see him when he wasn't "at home," like we're on a freaking play date. She kept telling me I'd thank her some day when she saved me from a life of single motherhood on welfare. Surprise! You can get pregnant right here in Sterling Creek. You'd think she would know that.

The drive to and from St. Cloud got more and more unpredictable as the weather turned cold and snowy, and there were a few weekends we were supposed to see each other and Scott couldn't make it. I fully admit that I thought about breaking it off several times, more because I felt like he should be able to enjoy being in college and not be moping around missing me or something, but then he'd have a break and he'd come home, and it would be just like it always had been between us.

We basically spent the entire summer after Scott's freshman year in college at the island. You know how he loved to build fires? At first he made coffee, but neither of us really liked coffee as much as we liked hot chocolate, especially without the little flavored creamers like at the Village Inn. But Scott could make a fire and he'd get the water boiling, and then he'd whittle up some little cocoa stir sticks. We had special tin cups that lived inside his little cook-kit, and we'd sit together in that one old chair and slurp our hot chocolate and I would say everything that was rattling around in my thoughts and he would listen, or seem like he was anyway. It was a comfortable thing, having Scott as my boyfriend for brief, intense periods (some far *too* intense, obviously), and then to have him gone, too. That was nice in its own way.

The next fall, when Scott joined the intramural hockey team, things got a little different. It was only a no-check league, and they didn't practice all that often, but I could feel Scott settling in with his own friends, his own life away from Sterling Creek. I convinced myself that it was good that he didn't call as much, didn't come home every single weekend he was able to. I didn't want him to be lonely. I wanted him to have a life there like I had with Dani and my other friends here, no matter how lame my life might have been. I trusted him, but I harbored no illusions either. We had already made it through a year apart, but high school was my world, and his was in college. I settled into the idea that it might not be forever, even though I truly loved him. That doesn't make me a bad person.

Dani covered for me to drive down to his games, but I was still separate from his friends there, and he didn't really talk about them either. I don't know, maybe I didn't want to hear it. We spent our time together talking about *us*, about our future, about how much we loved each other. Maybe we didn't have that much to say, truthfully. If I'd been allowed to visit him in St. Cloud more often, maybe it would have worked out differently. Maybe I would have been a part of their group, someone they would have embraced, but I sat on the bleachers alone and cheered for my boyfriend.

Scott's team won the playoff finals—a close, exciting game, and the stands had been pretty much packed, mostly with freshmen who lived in the dorms. It was a big deal, I guess. Scott didn't know I was going to be there, since I'd come the night before and it was hard for me to sneak down. Anyway, they won, and I waited there after the game, like a big dork, by the door to the locker room. I was experimenting even then with writing on my phone, and it was okay. Not perfect, but it made me unapproachable, which is how I like to appear. *Snarly*, says Dani's mom Janie. In fact, and this is a little weird, but that's my name on her blog. SnarlyGirl. She's written about raising Dani since Dani was about six years old, and retroactively shared most of Dani's known life before that, so I guess it's fairly natural that occasionally her daughter's prickly best friend plays a part in the drama that is "Raising a Rumpus," as Janie's blog is so adorably named.

So there I was, being all SnarlyGirl, typing away on my phone, when I realized the hallway outside the men's locker rooms in the basement of the intramural hockey rink was louder, more celebratory than usual. Sure, sometimes after a game Scott would be invited to go out for a burger with some of his teammates, but he always took me out instead. This time, though, there were like fifteen rowdy friends of his— mostly guys from his floor, but a few girls, too. One of them was a tall girl with one of those wiry, athletic builds. It's not like I wanted to be that way, but I admit to a sort of fascination with women whose body types are completely different from my own. I wasn't jealous, but I could tell just by looking at the easy way she stood there in that hallway that she'd been in and out of the corresponding women's locker rooms more times than she could count. This rec center was her second home. The group was talking loudly, their sentences running into the sentences of their friends, reliving great moments of the game, and when Scott emerged from the locker room, they erupted into a cheer that was so boisterous it completely embarrassed him.

"Shut up, you guys," was all he said, but he pushed through the center of the crowd with his head bent, shouldering his giant duffle. His hair was curly and wet from his shower. He was going to have frozen hair and a cold head. I slid my phone into my pocket and jumped off the little ledge where I'd been perched.

"Hey," I said, walking toward him. "Good game."

He looked up and the little smile on his face faded, just for a brief instant, and then lit up more purposeful and broad to let me know he was happy to see me. "I didn't know you'd be able to make it two nights in a row," he said.

"Took some planning, but Dani's the best liar ever." We stood, looking at each other for the slightest of beats, and then I jumped into his hug. It was good—he was my boyfriend. I wore his team colors of yellow and black.

"Do we finally get to meet your girrrrrlfriend?" said the athletic girl. I read her smile as genuine, but there were reservations. She teased Scott like they were friends. Good friends.

Two other girls lagged behind the rest of the group, giggling and pushing each other in a way that let me know they'd probably insulted me when the group walked by. Called me a creepy fat girl or some other thing a million people have said before. Girls like that are not known for their originality.

Within seconds, the group had closed in around us, even the giggly girls, who were extra nice when they introduced themselves like everyone did. Their names were a swirl of details I couldn't pin into my brain, but the tall girl, the one with the easy posture and the ponytail, her name was definitely Kendall. And she smelled like soap.

NOW

Joey and I stand in the concrete stairwell together to wait for my mom. Our voices echo.

"Do you think he and Kendall were..." He shakes his head.

I shake mine. "I don't know." And I really don't, but I remember that smell, and I know she was with him that day I drove down in secret, the day I told him. "I only know they were together. Close enough for me to smell her."

"Scott was a good guy," says Joey, and then I know he's done it, too. He's taken the Scott we know and relegated him to the past—a person we used to be connected to.

My phone buzzes. "She's here," I say, and then I don't know what comes over me. It's the same thing that's coming over everyone, I guess, and I grab Joey up in a hug. His shoulders are every bit as narrow as I thought they would be—he's a dried husk of a winged thing with dark pools for eyes. I'm so tired of this. Joey's surprised, but he hugs me back. We're all clinging to each other in search of comfort.

"I'm going to find out," he says. I'm not sure what to say, so I slip out the door.

Mom's tapping at her phone and doesn't seem like she's pissed she had to wait, so that's good. I give Joey one more little wave and then climb in, pulling my bag in over my lap.

"You're letting the cold air in," she says, but she's absent, her fingernails scraping across the screen of her own private world.

"What are you looking at?" I know she hates it when I invade, but I can't help it. Look at me, talk to me. I lean in.

"I need a new cardigan," she says, and sighs. "I guess *need* is too strong a word, but there's this thing I was going to maybe go see down in Duluth—" She stops, pushes me away. "I hate when you read over my shoulder." She tucks her phone back into the console and looks at me for the first time since I got in the car. "So what did the shrink say? Is it all your awful mother's fault?" She smirks, but it's a smile that doesn't conceal much of her insecurity.

"Whatever." I sink back into the seat, and this is the time, my chance. *I'm pregnant* would be all it would take, and what happened next would be on her. Would she slap my face? Kick me out of the house? Get pissed but stand by me? I think she'd eventually be on my side, that's the thing, even though I don't doubt there would be a lot of yelling, a lot of angry shit to wade through first. But would she sign the papers? That's what I want to know. Would she give me the choice to make?

"She told me to keep trying to remember, that's all." I say this instead of that other thing, for now. I tell myself maybe tomorrow. Maybe the day after that. One moment, and everything changes. A relentless storm of her anger with the hope of a quiet shore on the other side. Not tonight. I hold up the jar that I decorated with Celeste's glue gun. "I have a memory jar, but it's mostly empty."

"Whatever you end up remembering," Mom says, "knowing you, you'll be sure to write it down." She pulls away from the curb, and I can't tell, from her wry tone—from her sharp profile or her constantly drumming fingers—what she means.

THEN

(MEMORY JAR)

I remember the way he cried. I would expect a guy like Scott to cry when his grandma died or when his favorite hockey team lost—or won, I'm not really sure how sports stuff works—but I didn't expect him to cry when he moved away from home. I rode along on the day Scott and his parents took all his stuff down, which I was nervous about because I knew I was going to have to ride back up alone with his parents, and I didn't really know if it would be awkward or what. I mean, they were nice people, but a four-hour car ride can be a lot of conversation to maintain.

Anyway, his mom was hugging him obsessively and his dad was keeping busy building the loft bed and assembling a bookshelf, and it was weird because there we were, in the middle of his bedroom essentially, with his parents, and every time Scott even brushed against my arm, I jumped back like they were going to arrest me. But finally Scott was like, "Can you guys go take a tour of the campus or something so Taylor and I can say goodbye or whatever?" And I blushed at the whatever, but his mom gave him another teary hug and they promised to be back in an hour to pick me up.

It's not like we were going to have sex, okay? We were cuddling. We were sad. We'd seen each other every single day that summer except for two nights and three days when I was camping and canoeing with Dani and her moms in the Boundary Waters. I remember how he held my face in his hands—I loved the way that felt. His fingers touched my cheek so lightly, and his palm cupped my chin. He slid his hand up behind my ear and his fingers twined into the hair at the back of my neck. We looked at each other, and even through the blurry wash of my own tears, I saw his eyes fill up too. There wasn't enough time in all the world for us, then.

I wonder if he'd cry to leave me now. I wonder if I would have gone there for college the year after next. I wonder if we would have moved in together like we planned, or if we would have broken up and gone our separate ways, watched each other date other people from afar and sort of tolerated it, even though neither one of us would have liked it. I wonder if we would have had a baby, if we would have made that work. I wonder if I had killed myself, would he still be whole.

And I wonder about this Kendall person.

NOW

This morning Dani's car turns into the school parking lot, and although I make the obligatory noises of protest, I feel mentally prepared to enter the building. It helps that Mom took me out shopping last night for a cute new outfit, and I feel safe ensconced in a gigantic blue and orange silk scarf. The wind is cold but there's a heavy damp in the air, too, which feels odd for early January.

"I can do this," I say, and Dani pushes her shoulder into mine.

"Most obvious thing you've said, ever," she says, and bumps me again. "You can do absolutely anything, Tay."

"Cheesiest thing you've said, ever." I push her shoulder back with my own, and she holds the door to the school open for me to step through. I hesitate, taking in a deep breath and letting it out again slowly. Peace breathing, Dani's mom Janie calls it. Janie teaches yoga in the back of the yarn store Saturday mornings.

"The truth is always cheesy," says Dani. She gives me a pretend kick in the butt, and I walk in. I can do absolutely anything. Anything except remember the five most important minutes of my life. And my locker combination. I spin the lock quickly, hoping that my hands will automatically know where to stop, and after a couple of false starts, they do. Muscle memory. Dani's always talking about muscle memory, always studying with her hands waving all over the air. She connects the facts in her notes to little squiggly motions of her hands, and then when she's taking a test, you can see her at her desk, every so often, with her tiny hands twitching and swooping around her like hungry birds. She tries to get me to study with her like that, but I'd feel too silly moving around like that. She can get away with it, little miss cheerleader, captain of the danceline team. I'm the chubby girl with the glasses, writing an article for the school newspaper. My hands are a swarm of hornets dive-bombing a spilled snow cone.

Still, I wonder if I could get on a snowmobile again. If I could remember.

"Hey, Taylor," says a voice behind me. Cecilia comes in with a concerned look, reaching in for a hug. I spread my arms and lean in, wondering what this is, this lowering of my hug-walls. "You're looking amazing. Really. Are you holding up okay?"

I smile, feeling the tug of my lacerations as I do. "I'm all right, thanks. And thanks for the card." Cecilia's mom is my mom's gynecologist, which is a little weird, I admit. "And that crock pot full of…"

"Sloppy joes," she supplies, then gives me another hug before heading off to class. I reach into my locker for my stuff, wondering if I'll remember my schedule in the same way I remembered my combo. I'm going to have so much work to make up.

Between my locker and Dani's, a Cecilia-like scene replays about four thousand times—concerned face, compliments, hugs, smiles, thank you's for the flowers and the food and the gift cards and all the thoughts and prayers. Dani takes me by the elbow and escorts me, moving me among the curious throngs rather like a battering ram, and then drops me into World History with a tight squeeze of my shoulders. "I'll be back for you," she says. "You don't have to do this alone."

It's cool of her, but really, I'm fine, and I tell her that. "I'll see you at lunch." Here at Gordon High, we're allowed to leave campus for lunch unless we're in trouble, so in the winter Dani and I usually eat in her car while she drives around aimlessly. In warmer weather we might eat on one of the benches around Sterling Lake if there aren't too many geese, or at the old rocket ship playground, but in the winter it kind of sucks that neither of us lives close to school with a working parent. We could hang out at the yarn shop, but then Dani would be forced to eat her Internet-famous lunch, and we'd have to talk in the soft-wool hush of Fran's listening ears.

"You can do this," she says again, and she's gone. I slouch in the last desk and hope Ms. Smith feels like talking a lot today. Kids look at my face and quickly look away, but whatever. The face doesn't bother me anymore, except that the scab is starting to itch and it makes my skin all tight.

I pull out my notebook and think about the memory jar. What do I remember? What memory could get me a millisecond closer to the moment we hit that ice ridge? What are the options? Was it a fluke—a complete accident, a warping of time and space and speed and safety and Scott didn't realize he was moving that fast? Was there something he didn't see? Was I driving? Did someone tamper with the snowmobile? And then the worst possibility, the one that seems so likely, so probable: Did I drive the snowmobile into that ridge *intending* to crash? Did I want it all to be over, the decision made? My breath comes ragged, my vision narrowing with gray fuzz in the corners, and I should have known. Am I making a scene? Ms. Smith is standing beside me, bending down. She's making concerned sounds and nodding her head a lot, but her voice is really far away. I nod my head. She pats my arm and looks straight at me, but I barely see her.

There's this part of me that stands back and watches as I lurch up out of my desk chair at the same moment as Ms. Smith turns her back. I think I can see the crooked part on the top of my head, like through a crime-scene camera mounted high above the door. I stagger to my feet, and I wipe my sleeve across my face, and I have no idea why, but I just want to tell her. I want to tell everyone. "I can't remember it, okay?" The words spill out in my broken-voice need, and I can hear the buzz of whispers starting but I have to make sure they all know. I tuck my hands into the sleeves of my sweatshirt and hold my arms out stiffly at my sides. I'll break if anyone touches me. "I just can't."

I watch myself pick up the plastic jar, all covered with glue and plastic doodads, and press it tightly between my hands. "I'm going to get a drink of water," I say, squeezing the container. My elbows feel light, and they float upward. The plastic crinkles. "Please."

Ms. Smith waves me out the door with a worried look, but I make it out of the classroom, and by the time I hit the hall I feel better. Still, I suck deep gulps of air and pace the distance between this door and the next. It's everyone staring at me, that's all. Making me anxious. The calming breaths help, and I curse myself for making a scene. Now I'm going to have to walk back in there with everyone looking at me.

I pull out my phone and I'm not sure why. Celeste gave me her number in case I wanted to text her—she said she wanted me to, actually—but I don't know what to say. *Help me, I have high school?*

I have a missed text. At first my stomach plummets, thinking it's going to be another *Abortion is murder* message. The last one came after midnight and was a photograph of little tiny feet with a caption that said simply, *Adoption, not abortion.* Again, no match on the number, and again I wonder who would go through so much trouble to target me with pro-life messages.

The missed text is from Joey, and it's the weirdest thing because I totally have Joey's number in my phone from before the crash, from before all of this. My boyfriend's little brother, you know? I can't get used to how everything has changed, and no warning, no chance to get our lives in order.

Shes here u hafta come to hospital.

How can anyone even think that's language? I message him back with a picture of my WTF face. Then the phone rings, and it's him. I pick up, quickly, before Ms. Smith comes out here to check on me. "Ew," I say into the phone. "Why are you calling me? This is so archaic."

"It's Soap Girl," he says, and then he hangs up. *Shes in the building*, he texts.

Soap Girl? What?

Oh. *Kendall the Soap Girl? The one he ...* I pause, my finger hovering over the screen. Fuck it. I hit send.

Joey's text comes so fast, I'm not even sure he saw mine first. *She says she has to see you immediately. Coming to pic u up.*

Right now?

Ms. Smith comes to the door, smiles again at me with those understanding eyes, and I let her lead me back to my seat. The rest of the kids mostly look away, which is nice. I have to go to the hospital. Why the hell am I in history class? Joey's coming to pick me up. Everyone's taking a test, but I can't take a test. I'm still holding this memory jar.

THEN

(MEMORY JAR)

I remember the swimming lessons. This was after like ten trips across the lake in that stupid tippy-ass canoe that was not romantic. You can't kiss a boy in a canoe until you know how to swim, and anyway, I wasn't eleven anymore.

I trusted him. He had me lean back and let my legs float up and keep my head back and my shoulders flat on his palm. He supported me in the water like that until I could do it myself, until lying back on the water's surface was almost natural. But the second Scott walked away, I felt every bit of courage drain away from me, lost in water that suddenly felt cold and dangerous. I flopped around, my arms and legs thrashing, until Scott yelled at me—he actually *yelled*, "Get a grip, Taylor! You can touch!"

It was true; I had forgotten. We were in water about chest-deep for him, so plenty deep on me, but still, I could touch. It gave me a chill to think about how close to pure panic I was in that instant. I didn't like the yelling, even though I know he was trying to pull me out of my fear.

"I told you to trust me," he said, and he picked me up in his arms and I wrapped myself around him, warm in the cool water. I felt safe, and I did trust him. I know it sounds cheesy. The cheesiest. But I did, I trusted Scott, and everything that afternoon seems etched in my mind. That's exactly how it all is—all my memories from before the crash. Like an etching, a work of art careful and precise on my mental canvas. A story gone to press, ink to page. So what to do with these murky shapes beneath the surface, when the transparency of the past starts looking a little bit cloudy? I trusted him, that's the thing. What is all this about a soap-smelling girl?

NOW

I have to get to the hospital. I crumple the memory into a ball and deposit it into the jar, along with the others. Trust. My mom told me this morning I have to go to school. It's the only way I'll be able to get into a good college. I can't let anything slip. The teachers have been really nice to me, understanding everything I've been through in the last week, but that's only going to get me so far, and then the sheer volume of lessons I've missed is going to catch up with me. My phone vibrates in my pocket, and I wait until Ms. Smith is looking the other way before I slide it out of my pocket and look, expecting Joey.

It's Dani. *I'm getting close on the other issue, btw. You can relax.*

The other issue. My hand automatically slides over my belly. Relax, right. I have to get to the hospital, and the only way I can think of is to act like I'm the one with a medical emergency. There's got to be something I could fake, some kind of believable malady for a snowmobile crash survivor with a slight concussion to come down with several days later in class—no. Stupid plan. Anything I do that calls attention to my medical condition is going to be calling attention to the fact that I'm pregnant, and no matter how much they bust their asses on grades, teen moms don't usually win the scholarships.

I'm going to have to break loose, like in a prison movie or something. I'll get one of these kids to distract the guards and then I'll run, bullets bouncing in the dirt all around me. Ms. Smith's eyes keep landing on me—briefly enough so that it's not uncomfortable but deliberately enough so that I know she's looking out for me. Concerned face, ten o'clock. She perches on the edge of her teacher desk and sweeps her eyes across the class. Breathing. I count to five, count to seven, count to thirteen. My heart slows. It's the yoga that saves me—I've been rolling around on padded mats with Dani most of my life, learning to breathe even if I'm still the most unbalanced person in any room.

I raise my hand. "Ms. Smith?"

She's at my side in an instant. "Are you all right?"

"It's just ... I've been having these ... like anxiety attacks or something," I say. All the adults can understand anxiety, but especially teachers. "Can I go get another drink of water?"

She looks closely at me, and I'm pretty sure in that second she knows everything there is to know about me, and then she smiles. "Of course," she says, and hands me the hall pass.

I loop my hand through the lanyard and slip the pass

around my neck without breaking eye contact. I want her to know that this isn't something I can escape. Then I walk out of the classroom, snagging my bag and my tablet on the way out the door. I stop at my locker and successfully retrieve my coat and hat. From here it's only a matter of looking like I have all the right in the world to walk out of school. I dip my head and pull my hood up before I reach the outer doors, hoping nobody will ask me to sign out. Wind whips into me, and my phone vibrates again, Joey. *Parked by the gym.*

"Thank god, I was nervous I'd freeze to death," I say as he leans over the passenger seat to open my door. The inside of his car smells like lemons. "Do you *dust* your car?"

His response is to hit the gas and then the brakes, jostling me nearly off the front seat.

"Hey." His face is like a cat's, unreadable. I swing my legs all the way into the car and close the door properly. Part of me is thinking that Joey is actually partly crazy and is going to kill me the way his brother did not, and part of me doesn't care. Part of me would be relieved.

THEN

(TO JOEY)

I used to tease him about his indecision, give him grief about how I had to make all the choices all the time. He was a Pisces, you know. *Is*, I mean. Anyway, he couldn't make a decision to save his life, his two-fish mind always swimming like mad in opposite directions. You've seen what happens when you take him to a restaurant he hasn't been to before, a place where he doesn't have a "usual order." Torture. He stares at the menu in an agony of indecision, switching rapidly from choice to choice, and then he spends the whole meal regretting his choice. It made me absolutely nuts.

Once, I was helping him write a paper for his college comp class. It wasn't anything difficult, but Scott wasn't really the kind of guy who spent a lot of time writing. "That's your thing," he always said, and like a lot of people, he didn't really trust himself when he wrote. I sat on the foot of the twin bed while he swiveled crazily in the chair, balancing the laptop on his knees. We were alone in his room, a luxury born of Dani's ingenious lies, and I didn't want to waste the whole time on a stupid paper.

"It's just an argument," I told him, but the screen in front of him remained blank. "Pick something you're passionate about."

He leaned back in his chair so that his head pushed up against my arm. "I'm passionate about you," he said, and I guess it was a sweet thing to say, but for whatever reason it annoyed me, got me all prickly.

"So you don't have any opinions? You can't think of a single thing you stand for?" I pushed his head off me and sat up straight, getting angrier by the second but unable to pinpoint why. Scott raised his eyebrows, but I didn't stop. I frowned and stood up, started pacing the narrow space between the two beds and listing controversial subjects. "Immigration reform, gun control, biological warfare, privacy on the Internet. Vaccinations. Global climate change. Metal detectors in schools, whatever. Just pick a stupid topic," I said. I stopped in front of him, my hands on my hips. "You can't write a paper about me."

I don't remember much more of that night, only that moment of frustration when I stood in front of Scott and told him he had to find something other than me to feel passionate about, like couldn't he have written about hockey, or hunting, or something else he liked? It was claustrophobic, in a way, this idea that his world was narrowing down to a single focus, but a couple weeks later he showed me his paper. It was passable—it had a thesis and unobjectionable structure. But the thing that caught me off guard was the argument he'd finally decided on. The title of the paper: *Does True Love Exist?*

Scott's position was yes, and I was his proof. Even now, thinking of that paper embarrasses me.

NOW

Joey takes his hand off the wheel to light a cigarette, then takes his other hand off to roll down the window. I restrain myself from reaching over to keep us on the road, and then I notice he's using his knee to steer. "When I go to a restaurant," he says, offering me the smoke, "I order the special. I'm not picky." I wave my hand and shiver, cold and queasy in the cramped space of the car. I feel like I'm expanding, my molecules drifting apart, shifting states of matter in a moment. Taylor vapor.

"What's she like?" I hope he won't tell me too much. I can only handle little bits at once.

He doesn't hesitate. He's been waiting for me to ask. "She calls herself random," he says, and this little scoffing noise comes out of his mouth. "Like she's all bubbly and she has funny streaks in her hair and she prides herself on her randomness." He glances over at me. "That was basically her autobiography when we met," he says. He raises his voice to a silly falsetto. "Hi! I'm Kendall! I'm so random! I'm sorry about Scott, but honestly, I need to talk to his girlfriend!"

"Why would she want to talk to me?" My feet are up on Joey's dash right now, and I can tell by the sideways look he gives me that he's not really cool with it but he's not going to say anything because I'm a crazy pregnant girl or whatever. I hug my knees.

Joey's fingers tap on the steering wheel. "I don't have a clue, Tay."

Tay. I can't remember him ever calling me that before. Scott didn't, and his family doesn't. Only Dani, and occasionally my mom. "But seriously." I pull the engagement ring out of my pocket, still in its little bubble of cellophane. "Who is she, even? What does she want?"

He loved me. He wrote *term papers* about loving me. He wouldn't be with anyone else. I can't understand this.

Joey mutters, pulling the car into the hospital ramp and tearing the sunglasses off of his face as he does. He tosses them up on the dash and they slide all the way across to my side, every rattle a reminder of his anger.

I sigh. "Why are *you* so angry?" This girl isn't sleeping with *his* boyfriend. I didn't think that—I'm too tired for this. Fatigue hits, a sudden submerging as the car comes to a stop, and I lie back against the seat and close my eyes. "I don't want to see her," I say.

"Take your time," says Joey, and he snatches the sunglasses back off the dash—leaning across me all brusque and impatient in the process—and puts them on, reclining his seat and, presumably, closing his eyes behind the shades.

None of this should matter. I was about to break up with him. I blame it on the hormones, on this stupid pregnancy that makes me constantly want to puke. If he wasn't in this stupid coma, he could help me get this stupid abortion and he could go off with this stupid Kendall and be random to their little hearts' content.

I can't explain what it's like to not remember. When you're trying really hard to hear something, you can cup your hand around your ear, hold your breath, and listen. You can squint your eyes to see, or inhale through your nose to smell. You can even try really hard to relax, to the point that you can lower your own heart rate and blood pressure. But how do you try really hard to remember something that isn't there? I squint, and I hold my breath, and I *think think think*, but there's nothing I can hold on to. Every thought is slippery, and I can't hold on to what's real. I take out my memory jar and unscrew the lid. There's a soft smell of lotion or bath oil released with the lid, but there's no memory attached, and I try some more, to remember.

THEN

(MEMORY JAR, TOP SECRET)

I remember the night this all started like it was yesterday. No, like it was five seconds ago. This goes nowhere, and nobody sees this. As soon as I get home, I'll burn this paper and put the ashes into the jar and that will be all that's left of this story, that's how serious I am about this.

It happened in his truck, and if that isn't reason enough to get the abortion, I don't know what is. How do you even look your kid in the eye when you know he was conceived in the front seat of a Chevy pickup. I don't think we really planned to have sex in the truck that night, but it was cold, and we stopped to look at the stars. I was distracted, thinking about school and college and my stupid ACT test. We got out of the truck for a while and we tried to sit on the hood, hoping the heat from the engine would keep us warm, but even with a blanket down, the cold crept into our bones and eventually we shivered our way back into the cab. The stars were really beautiful, but I couldn't stop thinking about what it would be like if I followed Scott to St. Cloud and whether that was going to make everything work out happily ever after, and I admit there was this moment when I was like, what if I go to college with Scott and then he ends up being my only boyfriend and I marry him and what if he's the only one I ever kiss, the only boy I ever... I worried about those tests. I'm not good at math when I'm rushed, when I'm calculating out how many seconds per problem I have left. If I could get enough scholarships, I could go anywhere. I could do everything.

This was what I was thinking about, and then Scott started kissing my neck and I let out my breath and then sucked it right back in again, and I know I already said I would burn this, but I have to say it again, this goes nowhere but here, and I'm turning away so that Joey can't possibly read it even if he does have his eyes open under those awful sunglasses. He kissed my neck and that's my weakness, I can't even. He kissed me and I melted and pretty soon my breath was coming faster and my whole body moved to push closer to him. I slid my seat back and he climbed over the console and the gear shift, laughing as he tried to fold his legs into the tiny space. I picked up my knees and he fell against me, his weight between my legs. This wasn't our first time, just so you know. We had some things figured out—the fumbling of the condom wrapper, the arrangement of clothing. Our breath steamed the windows, and then it was over. My mind settled again on scholarship possibilities, and I smoothed down my skirt and pulled up my leggings. We didn't notice anything gone wrong. I mean, unless you count the fact that I was sitting there breathless and unfinished and distracted by school. When had sex become this quick, practiced thing that we did without thinking about it? I pulled my seat back up and was quiet, but Scott didn't notice my change of mood. He was jubilant and ready to go out and devour French fries dripping in mayo.

It was this stupid thing, in my head. I couldn't stop obsessing about the fact that we had most of our clothes on. I have no idea why it mattered, but I kept on seeing the image of him, lifting himself back over the console into the driver's seat, his boxers showing where his jeans were unzipped and, like, pulled down on his hips. He barely even had his pants off, and that bothered me. It was cold. We were sitting there in the truck, and even though we were parked at the edge of town, there were still people who could have happened by. And to think now that this is when it happened—that was the beginning? Doesn't an actual baby deserve something more than that?

Okay, that's it. That's what I remember. I went home that night and I couldn't sleep and I cried for no reason I could explain, making pathetic little sobs until finally my mom came in to my room and asked me if I was all right and gave me some tissues and a sort of hug. "It's just the night-sads," she said, and she went back to her bed looking a little pissed off, but her words helped. I slept after that, though the wanting -to-cry feeling has been with me ever since.

NOW

Obviously I'm here to see her, so I wrap up my whining session in the car and then Joey gives my hand a quick squeeze without looking at me, like he can pretend someone else is offering me this comfort. He offers to come in with me, but he understands this is between me and this Kendall person. He will wait for me in the car, my quick getaway prepared.

The automatic doors into the brain trauma ward always startle me, even though I've been through them a million times by now. The low hum they make as they swing wide is a menacing tone, at least today.

"Taylor," she says, standing up immediately when I approach the door of the family waiting room. She's several inches taller than me, with that easy athleticism I'd first noticed. "I'm so sorry to hear about Scott. Really, I don't even know how to express how much I feel for you, for his family."

She's so full of grace and ease. I open my mouth to ask a question, but she hasn't left me any opening, and I don't know quite how to go about asking her.

"Why are you here?" I finally say. It's not as though Scott's other friends haven't visited. They have, some from high school and some from college. They brought flowers and teddy bears and baskets and cards like everyone else. Some of them we knew and some were unfamiliar, but she's something different, and she knows what I mean when I ask.

She sinks to the waiting room couch, waving her hand to indicate that I should sit too. I stay on my feet for a moment or two longer to establish some things, but then I sit on the edge of the chair opposite. "We had ... I suppose I'll call it a relationship."

"A relationship?" I should be in history right now. No, Spanish. I should be thinking about heading to the library after school with Dani, maybe hanging out watching her cheer at practice. Any number of a million things besides sitting in a hospital waiting room listening to a girl tell me she was sleeping with my boyfriend. "I'm sorry, I can't do this. We met, once, right? At the playoffs game?"

She nods. "Scott talked about you all the time."

Scott didn't talk. "He never mentioned you." I still can't figure out why she's here, why she insisted on speaking with me. What does she want? Does she think that she's going to get a place to wait by his side, that she's going to be in there telling him stories like she's one of us—one of the people he loves?

Kendall pushes her streaky blonde hair back off her

face, twisting and retwisting the hair tie. "I can't believe I have to tell you," she says. "He told me he would tell you."

"Well, he didn't." I want to go back in time. I want to go back to that moment he hugged me and I want to say, *Stop. Who else have you been holding? Who else has a hold on you?*

Kendall twists her hands in her lap and then she looks up at me, and her eyes are all filled with tears. I'm queasy and evil, suspicious of a weeping girl. "It's my older sister," she says. "She and her husband tried for six years to get pregnant. He had a low sperm motility, but they tried everything, even in vitro. Nothing happened, and then my sister got uterine cancer." Kendall points to the little looped ribbon she has pinned to her shirt, and I wonder if she wears that all the time or only when she's trotting out some kind of sob story to explain to me why my boyfriend has failed to mention her. She cries then, full-on, no shame, not even wiping away the tears. Her eyes visibly redden right in front of me, and I'm a complete asshole if I still hate her.

"What does any of *this* have to do with your sister's uterine cancer?"

Finally, the girl has the decency to wipe her eyes with the sleeve of her sweatshirt. "She had to have a hysterectomy. They've exhausted all their medical insurance, with the fertility treatments and then with Kathryn's chemo and surgeries."

"But, Scott?"

"He should have talked to you about this."

"But he didn't." I'm confused, and I'm getting angry again, and there's this girl here, and there's a *relationship.* "Was he cheating on me, is that what you're trying to say?"

"Oh my god, this conversation should not be happening, okay? This is so random, I mean, what are the *odds*, you know? What happened on that snowmobile?" She looks up, dropping her hands, and her eyes are pleading with me, and they're so raw, so wounded. "I can't tell you. I can't say the words, knowing he didn't say them first."

I'm done with this conversation. I can't sit here anymore, listening to her tell me absolutely nothing. "Look," I say. "I don't have a lot of time. I basically ran away from school to hear what you had to say, and you apparently have *nothing* to say, so you can just—"

"He said I could have your baby," she says, her voice barely audible.

THEN

This one time I was at Scott's parents' house when a spring storm began, like they often do, with a sloppy rain. It fell on the roads and froze into a treacherous glaze as the temperature dropped—which was precisely when the rain turned over to snow. A flurry of disastrously large, heavy white flakes fell fast and thick, obscuring the slippery ice. It was Sunday night, and Scott's parents refused to let him drive back to St. Cloud even though his truck had four-wheel drive.

"Doesn't do a thing on ice like this," said his dad, standing at the window. "Gives you false confidence, that's all, and you still can't stop or turn on a sheet of black ice."

"Besides, with the snow drifting up on top like it's expected to do until after four this morning, they're saying visibility is down to almost nothing." Scott's mom leaned against his dad, and he tucked his arm over her shoulders.

Emily bustled around in the kitchen making cocoa, and Joey was playing the model teenager huddled up in his basement bedroom with the stereo shaking the floor beneath us. They all fit together there, picture perfect, and I felt so completely awkward in the middle of this functional family moment.

"I should probably get home before it gets too bad." I whispered it in his ear because I didn't want his parents to hear. I don't know, I guess I thought they would feel like they had to drive me or something because they're the parents. Never mind that we were practically grown, too. So I was leaning in on tiptoes, talking in his ear, when his parents stopped their murmuring at the window and turned to me in unison, like they've rehearsed this moment.

"There's no need," said Scott's mom. "You can stay here, and we'll get you to school in the morning." She smiled and basically headed straight for the linen closet. I'm pretty sure she had clean sheets on the guest bed before Scott's dad finished his next sentence.

"No way is there going to be school tomorrow," he said. "You know what that means."

At this point, I hadn't even said a word. Hadn't uttered a sound. I turned to Scott and raised my eyebrows, but he just grinned. "I don't know what that means," I said. I was thankful for their kindness, but, you know. Shouldn't someone at least ask me what I wanted?

"Don't worry about a thing," said Scott. "You'll see."

"It means you're going to learn how to play bridge," said Scott's dad. "And I'm not going to let you win."

NOW

I try to storm away. "You can't seriously expect me to listen to one more word," I say, but Kendall follows me into Scott's room, and I don't know what to do. I'm trapped, and again, I don't want to fight in front of him. I glare at her, but she sits down across from me, pleading with her eyes.

"We were close," she says, and her voice cracks. "He was going to tell you."

I can't speak to her, can't find any words in my head that are willing to line up into sentences that make any sense at all. Even so, I feel my anger transform into something much more difficult to hang on to. Silently, I pick up a deck of cards and start to shuffle. In my head I begin a thousand accusations, but I see the way she looks at him, and I know she loves him. Did he love her? I shuffle the cards close to Scott's ear, hoping the sound will trigger something in his consciousness, hoping he'll sit up and tell me the truth about all of this. I'm sure the school has called my mom by now. I deal out the cards and tell a story instead of talking directly to her, a story about the time I got snowed in overnight at Scott's parents' house and his dad tried to teach me to play bridge. We don't play bridge, this Kendall person and I, but after I finish the story, we do play a rather confrontational hand of rummy over Scott's still form.

"He said you could have our baby?" I put down a pair of aces.

"He called it the perfect solution," she says. She considers for a moment and then picks up my discarded eight. "I'm sorry, this is so random." Her eyes fill with tears again and she leans over him, rubs her hand across his arm, and it hurts me to know it feels slightly like a cushion. I don't want to believe this, but how would she know about the pregnancy if he didn't know her? If he didn't *confide* in her.

"You told him you'd *take* our baby." I can't fathom this. Why would Scott ever say that?

Kendall nods, and she swabs her face off with a soggy tissue while slapping down four eights and a trio of kings. "Rummy," she says.

THEN

I can't write about this Kendall person, not about what she said. I can't think about it without crying, and I don't want to cry around Joey. I need a memory. Something about Joey, maybe, like how he used to race motocross. I begged Scott to take me to a race but he said he couldn't watch his brother race. *It wasn't safe*, he said. He didn't like to drive things with a motor as much as things that were self-propelled. When he went to the island alone, he skated across the snow on his long, narrow cross-country skis, but together we mostly took Joey's snowmobile, and Scott never let me drive. I bothered him about it, that night. "Just let me drive, one loop around the island. I'll go slow," I said. I don't remember if he let me drive.

I don't remember don't remember don't remember.

Remember. Why can't I force my brain to go there? But there's something—a mosquito in my ear, if even a metaphor for a mosquito can exist in January. The fire had dwindled, but Scott kept stirring up the coals, coaxing more heat and light out of the little ring. "It's almost out, and then we can head back. If you get cold, remember you can wrap up in the wool blanket," he said. "In my pack."

He had a pack filled with every necessity, and he carried it everywhere. It didn't surprise me in the least that he was prepared for me to get chilly. "Let *me* drive home this time," I said, and I stepped toward him, putting my arms around him from behind. I can still feel his chest, the way my hands slid up and rested there, and even though I'd been waiting for my opportunity to break up with him, and even though I'd been ready to abort his baby, I still held him like that for a long moment, my face resting on his coat. He smelled like wood smoke and boy.

He shrugged—I could feel the muscles jumping in his abs—and sort of laughed me off. I understood, though. It was anxiety, and I'd seen it in other ways, too. Crowds, and sometimes even worse in wide open spaces.

"It makes me feel unconnected to myself," he said, in answer to my question, as if that was any kind of answer.

I pushed him. "You're only saying that because you don't trust me," I said. "You're sexist, and you don't let me drive because I'm a girl."

"I'm not sexist." He twisted out of my grip but caught

hold of my hands again, held me. He looked into my eyes, serious. "I don't let you drive because you're not *me*."

"Just let me try," I said, and I don't know if I want to remember what Scott decided.

NOW

It takes me three tries to get myself to open up the front door of my own house. So many questions are tearing me apart right now, and I have to pretend like nothing's wrong. Like the questions aren't about to fly out of my mouth at a moment's inattention. I slip into the kitchen and stand quietly behind my mom as she faces the sink.

It's obvious she knows that I skipped out of school again. I can tell by the set of her shoulders, by the fact that I'm studying her shoulders as she scrubs a frying pan that's been lying there in the sink for a week, the fact that she doesn't even turn around when I walk in the door. She's pretending I'm beneath her notice. "Hey, Mom," I say, and then I can't even shut my mouth before I'm spilling out too much. "I got a text from Joey that said this girl was at the hospital, this girl who knows Scott and her sister can't get pregnant."

Oh my god, what the fuck. Why did I say the word pregnant in front of her? Where exactly am I going with this line of thought? It's dead silent, but she turns around, soap suds dripping from her yellow rubber gloves onto the dingy gray linoleum. "Look, I know you were worried, but Joey thinks maybe Scott and this girl were sleeping together—"

"Taylor, what the hell." She makes her eyes all wide and kind of sticks her face toward me like she's been doing since I can remember, a menacing kind of way that never fails to make me curl my hands into fists.

This time I consciously relax my hands and take a breath. "I'm super tired and my life is in pieces, Mom. May I please just...go to my room?"

Mom narrows her eyes. "You'd better think long and hard about your attitude, missy," she says, and whatever, that's fine. She has her scripts and I have mine, and neither one of us has a picnic, let me tell you. She turns her attention back to her frying pan grease and her soap suds, and I slip into the sanctuary of my room and my creaky old bed and my moonrise window and my memory jar.

THEN

(MEMORY JAR)

Maybe it's a little bit funny that the only thing Scott and my mom agreed on was my writing—the fact that it was a waste of time and energy, that it isolated me and kept me from being ambitious enough. "You could do anything on earth," my mom said, scowling at me in the mirror. We were getting ready to go to some college fair thing at the high school, and she was already mad at me before we left because she didn't like the results of the interest inventory I took at school. "You could be a fancy-pants lawyer, make some real money and get us up out of all this." She waved her hand around our bathroom, like only my becoming a lawyer would get us out of the shitter. I stared myself down in the mirror and tried to remember that she was mostly acting like this because she hated going to the school, making small talk with the other parents, smiling at the people she knew had actual college funds set up for their kids. All that stuff was like torture for her. I didn't tell her about my plan to become a cardiologist. I told her I was going to be a poet, because a small victory can feel good even when you love someone.

"Why are you always scribbling in that silly book?" Scott would say, and he would tackle me to the floor, kissing my face, my hair, my neck, making me laugh like crazy until I couldn't remember why I'd want to put words in my silly book either. And maybe that was one of the reasons holding me back from choosing to go to St. Cloud with him. Having Scott around was bad for my writing. My poetry turned out all stupid and sappy, and I never got more than a paragraph into my fiction before he'd have me distracted. It's not that I was one of those writers, all tortured and sad all the time— someone who can only be inspired when they're in pain—but happiness made writing less vital to my overall survival. The worst part might have been that he didn't understand my poetry, not even the stupid, sappy ones. He didn't really try, waving his hands helplessly at the sight of a set of stanzas. It bothered me, but it was a small thing, really.

"You can write as a hobby." Mom leaned into the mirror, running a gloss over her lips and then wiping most of it off with a tissue. She pressed her lips together. "What are you going to do with an English degree, anyway?"

I didn't tell her about my vision of the future—the double major with pre-med, the internship and the literary magazine, studying anatomy and subbing poems and stories to journals and living in a funky apartment with Dani, with friends who drank coffee and talked about ideas and had formulated opinions about gender and feminism. A stethoscope around my neck, making rounds. A chapbook of poems. Watching open heart surgery at the elbow of an amazing surgeon. An anthology of short stories that would get me a novel deal. Dani and I talked about it all the time, and it felt anything but unrealistic. It felt like the inevitable truth of our future, but I knew that if I spoke the words aloud to her, all wisps of possibility would vanish. The future could be fragile like that.

It was always a little bit uncomfortable to me that a tall, blue-eyed hockey player with broad shoulders and a shy smile wasn't automatically in my vision for my future. Dani was, and poetry and medicine, but not Scott. It's not that I couldn't find a place for him there, if it turned out that way, but it certainly wasn't an automatic.

"What do you even see happening to us?" Scott asked, that night on the island. This was before the ring appeared, before the flames started to die. It wasn't a desperate question, but a curious one, and I wanted to answer him in a way that would make both of us happy. I still cared about that, even though I was about to break up with him, but here he was making me cocoa with a little whittled stir-stick and there was no way off the island without him. I shook my head. "I'm sorry, Scott, but that's the least of my worries right now," I said.

At that moment, or before that moment, was he promising this girl I didn't even know that she could take our baby?

Why would he ask me to marry him, then? They were *close*. Why didn't he say anything? Why did he leave this mess for me?

NOW

Days pass with no more signs of increased consciousness, but no negative changes either, and the hospital staff moves him again, farther from the nurses' station and closer to the rehab center. I send messages online to Scott's roommate and two of his hockey friends asking what they know about this Kendall person, who has not shown up at the hospital since the bizarre game of rummy. Emily has promised to let me know the instant she sees or hears anything from Kendall, but I don't tell her why, not yet.

The mystery texts have stopped, but Dani hasn't had any more luck with the other plan either. Eight weeks. I have to have this taken care of before week twelve, before the first trimester is over. I'm still queasy all the damn time, but I'm keeping food down, so I haven't lost any more weight. Assignments are given and are due, and I have to work hard in school to keep up, even with the extra help and forgiveness and Ms. Smith's kind face especially. Even now, though, my brain can go funny—kind of slow and sleepy-like, and I keep trying to remember what happened.

"How did you sleep?" Dani turns down the music when I get into the car, and she makes me lift up my sunglasses so she can look at my eyes. "Your pupils are responsive to light," she says, before I can even shrug. Everyone we know is becoming an expert on head trauma.

"I'm good." Even though she's not looking at me now, I shrug because that's what it feels like, this waiting. "I wrote a poem." It's not a nice poem, but I read it to her anyway, and then I crumple it up and put it into the memory jar, which is slowly filling up even though I'm no closer to remembering the crash than I was a week ago. At the bottom of the jar, there's a thin layer of ash. My face itches, and I resist the urge to claw at the scab.

"It makes me feel all worried and stuff," she says. She spins her hands on the steering wheel in time to the soft reggae music in the background. "All that stuff in there about swallowing pills. Are you all right?"

"It's not about suicide," I say. "I promise. It's a survival story, like I said."

"Okay, then. If you're sure."

"I'm not going to kill myself."

"No killing," says Dani, but then there's a stupid awkward silence and the seat belt presses against my abdomen like a noose.

THEN

(MEMORY JAR)

Tonight I keep
imagining the tragedy
the wash of tingling panic
beat—the stop the start of casualty
the dizzy curl of pain behind
the sinking rising surge
of errors and questions
heroic instances or dumb paralysis
it's all the same

Already I can feel
the sodden tissues feel
the blurry nestle of pills swallowed
at someone else's insistence
the walls of my will wearing to dust
and my anchored eyes collapsing
into pits like sunken treasure—
the tales that are told

Survival stories

NOW

Still no word from Kendall or any of the people I messaged asking about her. None of my limited searches—I don't even know her last name—are turning up any information, and I start to think sometimes that I imagined her. It's worse when I get myself convinced that I've imagined all of this, when I come out of the fog of my brain and recognize reality.

It's not that I would ever give the baby to this Kendall person, or to her sister, for that matter, even if Scott were to wake up right this instant and tell me it's what he wants. Still, there's this part of me that wants to let this pregnancy's future be determined by chance. I don't know what that says, that there's a part of me that basically wants my free will taken away. This part of me has seriously considered letting the outcome of Scott's consciousness determine my fate—I could draw up a chart with rows and columns, matching up with different outcomes. *Remembers pregnancy exists AND can utter complete sentences? Have the baby. Remembers pregnancy BUT has dramatic personality change? Terminate.* Look, I know that sounds horrible, and I suppose it is, but I guess I'm not the first girl in the world to feel terrified and unprepared for motherhood.

I stare at Scott's face, thinking of a baby who will have his blue eyes—eyes I could never see again. He was good at eye contact, you know. Not only with me, though his gaze could melt me right down to my middle under the right circumstances. Scott looked at people, and something kind of quietly assertive in his eyes would be like "I see you, and I value what I see." I miss that look, and I wonder if this kid would inherit it, even if its father never opened his eyes again. I wonder what it would inherit from me.

Ms. Smith gets me a spot at the tutoring center for calculus, which is pretty cool of her since she's not even my advisor or anything. The guy whose sad job it is to help me takes a shaky breath before every phrase while he explains each type of problem, and he keeps wiping his hands on his jeans like that will disguise the fact that his palms are damp. His handwriting is meticulous, and I find myself looking at his hands kind of a lot, to be honest. Dani has cheerleading practice, so it's just me and Eric. I like him. He doesn't talk much beyond the necessary, and he has nice breath—cloves and orange, like a fancy grandma's closet. I mean, it smells better than I'm describing it. So Eric is all whispering about cosines or binomials or derivatives—something, honestly I have no idea. It's, like, statistically impossible to pay attention to calculus when you're pregnant and you were supposed to be a heart doctor and your boyfriend's in a coma and maybe your entire relationship was a lie and you're thinking about another boy's breath and your best friend is doing splits in midair and it's four o'clock and you wonder if the office lady with the kid in dance line or whatever is still there selling chocolate bars because there is *no way* you're going to make it until dinner. So Eric elbows me, and I turn away from the window where this very picturesque snow was falling.

"Do you want to"—shaky breath—"get some pizza?" he says, and I think holy shit, is he asking me out? What is this? But then I realize that all the tutors are packing up their stuff and everyone's getting together as a big group. "We"—shaky breath—"usually go out on Friday."

A few minutes later and I'm riding shotgun in my tutor's station wagon, and then suddenly I'm smiling in a corner booth, drinking a bottle of root beer and watching a bunch of smart kids throw darts and play Ping-Pong and pinball at Thrasher's Pizza.

Mom orders pizza from Thrasher's sometimes, but she usually gets it as take-out, and she picks it up because she stops at the liquor store on her way. Scott and I never went there, and Dani can't go there because she has the most ridiculous crush on the owner's kid and does nothing but blush and giggle the whole time we're there. It's a busy place tonight, not just the usual stoner crowd and the jock crowd but other crowds, too, like us. Eric sits beside me in the booth, and I see how sorry he feels about me and my plight. To him, I'm the girl whose boyfriend is in a coma, or maybe the girl who almost died in the snowmobile crash. The girl who is hopeless at calculus, definitely.

"So Taylor," he says. "Are you doing okay? Like in life, not in calc."

I laugh and look away. "Yeah, because we both know the status of calc." I'm too cool for this conversation. I grab my bottle of root beer, intending to take the most nonchalant of all drinks, but fail with a spectacular crack of the bottle against my front teeth.

"Ouch." He winces, then peers at my mouth in concern. "I think you might have chipped it."

My hand flies up to cover my mouth as my tongue explores the edges of my two front teeth and finds a sharp place where there used to be smooth enamel. Oh my god. I did not just chip my front tooth. Then the pain hits, and I can't even believe it. Not only did I chip my tooth, but I seem to have broken it in a way that's serious enough to need dental attention. At six o'clock on a Friday night, while I'm at a tutoring pizza party. *Before* I've eaten any pizza, for fuck's sake. "Bad news," I say, around my hand. I feel so dumb. I tap my hand, the one that isn't clapped over my mouth, against the table, my fingers drumming out a nervous rhythm.

"Let me see," and he tries to gently peel back my hand, but I shake my head.

"I can't," I say. "I'm afraid part of my tooth is going to fall off or something." The drumming speeds up, the chorus in my head repeating *dumb dumb dumb dumb.* "It hurts." *So so so dumb.* Now I'm going to have to text my mom to come get me, and she'll be pissed as hell because she's already going to be in her yoga pants with her hair all up in a ponytail and her makeup scrubbed off and her glasses on. I mean, she's going to be pissed that I need, like, emergency dental surgery outside of the normal hours and probably outside of our lame insurance plan that really only covers things like one cleaning every year or something.

"I can drive you home," says Eric, and his breath doesn't shake.

"You don't have to do that," I say, my hand still over my mouth. The pain seems a little less. Maybe I can wait until Monday, if I eat soft foods or chew with the back of my mouth or something. "I'll text my mom, or maybe Dani can come get me."

"I don't mind bringing you," he says, and it's tempting, even if he wants to talk about awkward things like how I'm really doing, in life-not-calc. I shrug but I also nod, and Eric smiles, pats my shoulder like a friend, and goes to talk to one of the guys at the counter. My tongue won't leave my tooth alone, and I can tell that it's bad, like I'll-probably-die-in-my-sleep-by-choking-on-the-missing-piece-of-my-front-tooth bad.

"It's all set," he says, tossing his keys lightly in the air. "I paid for your drink, even though you didn't get a chance to drink much of it."

I sit in his car, holding a chunk of snow wrapped in one of Eric's old T-shirts up to my mouth. "I feel like the world's biggest idiot," I say, pressing the cold snow gently against my upper lip. The ache from the tooth seems to have spread across my entire face, and I don't know how I'm going to sleep.

"Yeah," says Eric, and then he shakes his head and laughs.

"I mean no"—shaky breath—"you're not an idiot. This is terrible timing, though."

I nod, but then I realize he probably didn't see me in the dark and while he's driving, so I find my voice. "I'm going to try to make it until Monday."

He glances over. "I know I only saw a glimpse," he says, "but it didn't look like you should wait." He looks back at the road, and his voice gets stronger. "Dentists can do good work with that bonding stuff. Nobody will be able to tell."

I haven't looked in the mirror yet, but I know it's not going to be a simple fix, from the way it feels on my tongue. If I look, I'm afraid I'll cry and that's not going to happen. My fingers are drumming again—*dumb dumb dumb dumb*—solid thuds of self-loathing on the armrest. "I can't do this." I can't pretend I'm not freaking out.

"You'll be okay," says Eric. "The dentist will fix it. You can suck back the laughing gas and not feel a thing."

I lean back against the seat so hard I'm afraid I'll break it. "But I'm pregnant," I say, my voice barely above a whisper, and it feels so ridiculously strange to tell someone—to tell a virtual stranger—that I start to laugh and then I do cry and there are tears and snot and a little bit of blood on me, and I bet Eric is really sorry he insisted on driving me home. "I don't think I can have laughing gas." I giggle through the words, finding it utterly hilarious that I'm laughing while lamenting my inability to have laughing gas. Tears are streaming out of my eyes, and I no longer have any idea which are tears of laughter and which are tears of fuck-my-life.

"Whoa." Eric draws a couple shaky breaths and keeps his

eyes on the road, mostly. "Listen, Taylor, when I asked if you were okay, like ... this is sort of the kind of thing that might make you say no. You know?"

I wipe the last of the tears away, though I'm still giggling and maybe hiccupping, too. "I think he might have been cheating on me." Peace breathing. I pull myself together.

Eric slows the car, puts on his signal to turn into my street. "So is it true, that stuff people have been saying?" He parks and lets the engine idle. "I mean, I'm sorry. You can tell me it's none of my business, but Taylor, are you"—shaky breath—"*are* you thinking about suicide? This pregnancy, I mean—does anyone know?"

I'm still buckled in, held to the earth and the seat of Eric's station wagon by nylon straps and metal clasps. My fingers rest on the belt but make no move to release me. "You know," I say. "Dani knows. And Joey knows now, but things with Joey are complicated, I'm not even sure." What does he mean, everyone's been saying? "Have people been saying I'm suicidal?"

He keeps his eyes straight ahead, and I see his throat bob as he swallows, while he decides how to respond. It's a very uncomfortable moment. "It's just ... there was a post, I think, I'm not sure where it showed up first, some person who was friends with a friend or something, I don't know. They posted about how they were super worried about you, that they thought you were probably deeply depressed and suicidal. They said you tried to jump off a bridge or something, and then when you chickened out at that, you crashed the snowmobile, you know. To kill yourself."

"Wait, what? This is all online?" Nobody knows about

the jumping except Dani and Scott. I haven't told anyone else. Mystery posts from a friend of a friend? *Unless he told someone.*

I unbuckle the clasp and my seat belt slides off one shoulder and bumps softly into the housing above my shoulder. "I can't remember the crash," I say.

THEN

(TO ERIC)

I remember the moon. There wasn't a full moon, but it wasn't far gone either. There were shadows, you know? I want to believe that I remember riding on the back, my face buried in the back of Scott's down vest, but I also have a possible memory of learning to work the throttle. But I can't tell where that memory fits, which one is true and which is one I only want to be true.

I remember the cold. I remember the moon. I remember begging him to let me drive, but I can't remember his answer. Again this haunting image lingers around me like a cloying smell, the press of handlebars against my belly, the blood in the snow. It was a lot of blood. And none of it was real. But what if, like everybody thinks, what if that image was my dream, my wish? What if it *was* me who crashed the machine, and what if I did it because I imagined myself dying, of course my belly bearing the injury—the pregnancy I wanted to be rid of.

I remember the moon, the sparkle of snow in my eye-lashes, the deep blue-black of the sky. I remember a crunch. Or nothing. What if I did this?

NOW

"You don't need to worry about what ifs," says Eric, but he has no idea how many what ifs I can worry about at once.

"Would the police use that kind of social media post in their crash investigation? If they ruled it an attempted suicide, does that mean insurance won't cover the bills?" This is ridiculous.

Eric drums his fingers on the steering wheel. "I don't think they can base their investigation on hearsay or whatever. Internet gossip."

"But they could take me in for questioning. They could ask me if I tried to kill myself. Or they could find this mystery person who seems to know so much about my life and my mental state." I remember those cops, and I wonder if they're still investigating. What do they know about the cause of the crash? He doesn't say anything for a while. I think about texting Celeste, and my tongue gingerly pokes at the jagged tooth, and I wonder whether Eric will tell anyone about my situation. I realize that I don't really care if he does—on a scale of one to boyfriend-in-a-coma, more rumors barely register.

"I don't think anyone's going to be looking to interrogate you, Taylor. Everyone knows this is a terrible time. Everyone's praying for you, and sending good vibes, whatever, you know? Even the drama talk at school is couched in the language of concern. Everyone is *so worried about you omigod.*" He makes his eyes wide and concerned.

"You're a really nice guy," I say, and if I didn't have my hand over my mouth I'd even smile at him. "Thanks for bringing me home."

"Good luck with the dentist," he says, and he waits until I fit the key into the lock of my kitchen door and even a moment after I close it behind me and turn on the bright yellow light of the kitchen. He backs out onto the street and leaves in the direction he came from originally, and I shed my winter gear and pull a chair up to the counter, my head heavy in my hands, delaying the moment I'll have to wake up my mother.

THEN

(MEMORY JAR)

I remember the time I came home from school to find my mom and Scott sitting here, drinking coffee in my kitchen. The pot was still burbling, little hisses on the hot plate to let me know that they hadn't been sitting there long—maybe long enough for the pot to brew but not enough to linger over their second cups, not enough to talk about anything serious.

So this is a thing, one thing I navigate. My mom. She's good to me, and she loves me fiercely. Like she would fight for me. But she also fights against me, there's the rub.

"She's so irritable," said Scott, "so angry all the time," and that was true, especially the pieces of her that he saw, at least partly because he irritated her. He didn't know how to read her, and he would keep on pushing, asking questions.

I knew how to listen for the sound of her key rattling in the lock, a stomping of snow off her boots on the mat, all these clues to what I needed to do—who I needed to be.

"Hey," I said, walking in the kitchen door. It was surprising to see them together, but worse, my mom's face was unreadable, the laughter clearly fake but concealing an expression I couldn't get a fix on. Something that was turning into angry. "What's going on?"

Mom shot me laser-beam eyes. "I suppose you think this is funny," she said.

I wasn't even smiling, not really, or at least I wasn't trying to. My face only betrayed me when she yelled at me, the corners of my mouth twisting up every single time even though I knew how much it pissed her off. "What's funny?"

"Because I know I find it *hilarious*," she went on, holding her phone screen in front of her, "having to work twelve hours a day and coming home to find that you not only neglected to leave out money for the cell phone bill, but that you have *seven hundred* text messages this month. That's four hundred over our plan, Taylor."

Scott and I exchanged a look, and then he winked at me in a way that made it impossible to stop the smile creeping over my face. I hoped she couldn't *read* the messages in addition to counting them. "Is that what the two of you were discussing? My phone bill?" It was typical for her to be worried about bills, but I had the money saved up from babysitting every Saturday night and watching the psycho-sisters next door while their mom gave piano lessons in the basement. "I forgot to put the money on the counter, that's all."

Mom rolled her eyes, took a sip of her coffee. "Of course we weren't talking about your damn phone bill," she said. "We were talking about sex."

She watched my face, waiting for the shock. She loved to shock me in an attempt to gain information from me, but I was good at keeping my secrets. I raised an eyebrow.

"Whatever."

"No, really, I think we kind of were," said Scott. "In a roundabout kind of a way."

"Gross," I said. "More Planned Parenthood stories?"

Mom laughed, and I could get a better grip on her mood. Not as angry as she seemed at first. "There was a protest," she said, and then paused to take another drink of coffee, giving me a chance to be appropriately intrigued, which I was. "Scott and I were talking about this woman, a part of the protest, who kept talking to me like I was someone going into the building to have an abortion. She was pleading with me and trying to shame me, showing me pictures of fetuses. It was awful." She shook her head. "It's not like anyone's performing abortions in the office building, good grief. The clinic doesn't even have a bathroom of their own, much less facilities for ... medical waste."

"Does that kind of thing happen often?" asked Scott.

"Protests?" Mom set her cup down. "Sometimes. That one church does a monthly sign-waving event, but they mostly stay out by the street with their signs, nothing you have to walk past while they yell at you about god and babies. No weird women with severe faces and gory photographs actually touching you as you try to get by. She grabbed hold of me, Taylor, like this." My mom dragged on my arm, and I flinched at her touch. I couldn't imagine what would possess someone to take hold of my mother like that. "These people were different from the Joyful News people," she went on. "I didn't know any of them, which means they came from somewhere else, on a bus full of Life Riders or some such."

Scott shook his head. "I don't agree with their methods, but I understand the sentiment." He shuffled through some papers on the counter. "I mean, look at this stuff. It makes me feel terrible to even read it, and the pictures... ugh."

"Yeah, look at this, Taylor, look at this propaganda." She took the papers out of Scott's hand and shoved them into mine. "This is the kind of thing that woman was sticking in my face, and I'm just trying to get to work, which, you know, has no effing connection to abortions." She stabbed her finger at the diagram of the incision on the back of a fetus's head and the gory text describing this procedure and made a sound of disgust. "As if it isn't depressing enough to be a receptionist in the office of a failed therapist."

"Failed?" I pushed the awful brochures away, no longer hungry for an after-school snack, that's for sure. "What do you mean by that?"

Mom sighed, nodded to Scott like he already knew about this part. "This is the other part of what we're talking about," she said. "The practice is closing at the end of March."

"Whoa." This was big news. "Were you planning on telling me?" Nice that she was telling my boyfriend secrets that affected my future without telling me.

"It's not like it's tomorrow," she said, and then shook her

head. "I mean, the only reason I know this far in advance is that I'm in charge of making all the arrangements for notifying our long-term clients to find a replacement. We'd close immediately, but it's not fair to the kids who need us."

Scott shifted on his stool, and the leather seat made a particularly loud sound, breaking into the tension. We all laughed, a little halfheartedly.

"Anyway," said my mom, "there's a lot going on right now, and I'd really appreciate it if you would remember to pay your phone on time." She finished her coffee and left her mug on the counter when she went upstairs.

NOW

Thinking about those brochures makes me think about that woman at the protest or whatever, the woman who grabbed my mom's arm. Would it be possible for an organization like that to hack into phone numbers of people in the Planned Parenthood building somehow? Or maybe it's more random than that—I don't know how all that big data works. Maybe the texts aren't related to my mom working in the same building, maybe all of this is simply a part of increased protest activity in the area. It could be a complete coincidence that I'm pregnant. Maybe a lot of people are getting spammed with pro-life texts. I scroll through them, wincing at the images, noting that none of them include my name or any other specifics. I take a deep breath, and the air passing over my tooth fills my whole head with pain.

I need to go to the dentist. The dentist is going to need to do reconstructive work, probably requiring some kind of anesthesia. I spend a minute or two searching "pregnant and dental work" on my phone, which I probably should not do again, and for whatever reason the term "crosses the placental barrier" makes me so queasy I nearly throw up. I would throw up if I weren't afraid of losing the rest of my tooth in the process. Instead I perch on the stool and write out my memory for the jar, even though I can't really figure out how such a memory is going to help me remember the crash and who caused it. Maybe that's not even the point of the jar, but all I know is that it's helping, in some way, all this remembering.

The dentist is going to need to know that I'm pregnant, right? I mean, all the medications they might give me, even the oral numbing stuff, can apparently affect the baby, and I think I'll have to sign something, or my mom will, that says I'm not pregnant. Even if I don't plan to stay pregnant. Do I? I think about those pictures, that awful pro-life propaganda my mom showed me that day, and I wonder what she thought of it, really. Not of the protest, but of abortion. Not the awful pictures of babies with the brain incisions either. This isn't like that. I'm barely over eight weeks, probably less, since I took the test right after I missed my period. It wouldn't be like that. This baby isn't a baby yet. It's just a glob of cells. The *potential* of a baby.

And then there's this Kendall situation. For a millisecond, let's consider this to be true, that Scott and Kendall were really *close*, that he went to her and told her about the pregnancy and she told him about her sister—or maybe he already knew, if they were so close—would he ever have offered the baby to her family without telling me? Even if it seemed like a brilliant solution, would he have promised her that and then kept it a secret from me? And *then* asked me to marry him? And who *is* she, even?

Once again I flip back to the string of mystery texts, thinking about what Eric said, the person who posted the rumors about me attempting suicide. Is it *her*? And if Scott told this Kendall person, who else did he tell? It's disturbing. What if Scott wakes up and doesn't remember? What if he never wakes up to say, one way or another? Why do I have to deal with all of this without him?

I hold my phone in front of me, switching from one app to the next, like something is going to change. Some magical post will make everything—chipped tooth, fetus, coma—disappear. Instead it only becomes immediately apparent to me how visible it is. Maybe not the baby, not yet, but my whole feed is choked up with people telling me how much they care about me, how much they want me to get better, inspiring quotes about depression, a few posts blaming me and calling me selfish, telling me if Scott dies I will be his murderer. I wonder if Dani is seeing this. There's no way she's the one who told, absolutely no way. But that's the thing, the one thing that presses my heart into a corner, because I thought there was no way Scott would ever betray me either, and now there's no way to find out.

They say there's a limit on the number of decisions you can make. I guess even small choices can add up all throughout your day and then you get this thing called decision fatigue. It affects your ability to be rational, essentially. Sugar fixes it for a while, but of course sugar doesn't have the best track record when it comes to endurance, so you run out of logical choice by the end of the day. Choice—this is the word I grapple with right now—and it begins with whether or not I can tell my mother I am pregnant.

Time slows, syrupy thick and scary, and the house makes night sounds, the furnace kicking in from somewhere deep beneath me in the basement, in the bowels of our home. I wait for a sound from my mom, for a sign that will tell me what I should do, what I should choose. It's too late for this shit, you know? I chipped my fucking tooth, I can't even believe it. I stand up, and on a whim I pull open the junk drawer in the corner where the counter turns from dining room into kitchen. The pamphlets are still there, full-color and gruesome. Designed to make this choice equate to being a murderer. For a moment I can't move, but then I pull them out, slow and deliberate, and I stack them into a neat pile in my hands, aligning their edges just so. The paper is thick and waxy between my fingers and I hold it for a little while, pinched between my thumbs and fingertips, and then I twist and tear, top to bottom. I spin the pages and tear again and again, until the paper babies cannot be further dissected— until I cannot quite get a full breath in my lungs. It's too late, and I am fatigued, and I broke my tooth and now I have to go in there, to her bedroom, and pull her back into this world to say—what? What will I tell her?

I can't throw away the pieces, so I place them back into the drawer. The hall is painted a pretty midnight blue, with silver sparkles painted into the wall going up the narrow wooden stairs toward my room in the attic. It's one of my favorite places, our entryway, and I linger here longer than I should. My feet drag across the hardwood toward her bedroom, but before I get there, the knob turns and she faces me.

"How was pizza?" she says, and it's hard to read her, despite all my practice.

"Mom?" I'm waiting, stalling. I need more information. I tip my head a little to see what kind of show she was watching. There's a lot of difference between lying in bed watching reality TV about wedding dresses and lying in bed watching one of those made-for-TV movies aimed at making people cry. My tongue can't stay away from the crack in my tooth, and I fight the urge to hide behind my hand when I talk to her.

"I'm glad you got out for a while, something normal," she says, with a long sigh. She's sad, then, kind of mopey but not angry. This will work.

"Mom?" I'm not sure what I'm going to tell her until the words are out of my mouth. "I've got a little problem."

Her mouth pulls in a bit but her eyes are still soft, concerned, and dismal. "What's the matter?" She doesn't reach for me, but she doesn't pull away either.

I could say anything. I could tell her, and I think she would hear me. *I'm pregnant. I'm suicidal. I might be a murderer.*

"I . . . chipped my tooth," I say. "I haven't looked at it yet, but it feels bad." My lungs still struggle for oxygen.

"Oh, Taylor, *honey*. Let me see." She leans into Emergency Mom mode, and it's exactly the mom I need right now. It's going to be okay. I breathe out, and I feel so much anxiety exit my body with that air, it's unreal. Her hands gently pull open my mouth, and her reaction is controlled, professional. "It's pretty bad, but don't worry. I've got this," she says. "I'm going to check first with this new dentist I heard about." She hesitates a moment, then scrolls through the contacts on her phone.

"Instead of the regular dentist?" It seems like someone with my records and stuff would make more sense.

She doesn't look up. "I've got this," she says again. "Dr. Zimmerman will be great, trust me."

Trust her. She's managing all of this so well, I'm ready to tell her about the pregnancy and go along with whatever she tells me to do, that's how tired I am of making decisions. But then I let that thought roll in the bowl of my brain, colliding with the thought of once again giving up my free choice, which makes me angry at myself, which makes me come to my senses again and say no way in hell am I going to tell her. I'm not going to leave my future up to the whims of a woman who once confined me to my room because I refused to remove all the Oxford commas from my English essay. I'm not going to decide what to do with my potential baby based on what Kendall says or on the random chance of Scott's recovery or under the influence of creepy dead baby pictures from a person too chickenshit to sign their texts with their name. I am going to make the best decision for my life, and for this potential person's life, too.

Dani said not to worry. She's working on a way to get around the parental notification issue, and as soon as she does, I'll be done with this. Before ten weeks, before those awful little feet. I can't have a baby, and I can't give my baby away to a girl who probably slept with my boyfriend. I can't let my mother decide, no matter what she seems like right now. I want more for my child, when I'm ready to have one, than a life of wariness.

I can't have a baby. I'm going to medical school and becoming a renowned writer, simultaneously. I'm going to break up with Scott and never have sex again. At least, not in a car. Not without candles and music and soulful gazing into each other's eyes. Not with fries dipped in fucking mayo, that's for damn sure.

She chose to have me. Because that's the other argument, right? If my mom had an abortion, I wouldn't be here. And aren't I a gift to this world? A *life*, right? But really, what would be different if I weren't here, if my life had been scraped out before I had a chance to become an individual who would regret not being around? Maybe my dad wouldn't have taken off. Maybe they would have stayed together long enough to develop into emotionally mature people who could someday have raised a functional family, or maybe they would have split up in a completely normal way and gone on to have a number of possibly-positive and possibly-unhealthy relationships with unknown outcomes and maybe my mom would have gotten her degree in whatever she was interested in before getting pregnant and wouldn't have ended up being a receptionist who sits and watches teenage girls carry their pee down the hall to the Planned Parenthood and then, even if I, by some chance of fate or through intelligent design of our universe, were to be born to my mother in a different future, I would have been able to get on birth control like everyone else and would have avoided having to make this decision myself.

They'll call me a slut. I know, it's not an original insult, and it's stupid that the word "slut" becomes the default insult for any girl for any reason, but they'll call me a slut, and I can't help it if that's hard for me to face. They'll talk about me and get quiet when I come close, and by next spring, I won't be able to hide it ... is it so terrible of me, as a teenager, to be scared of that?

"So, okay." Mom waves her hand in front of my face to get my attention. "Doctor Z is going to open up for you right away in the morning, but she said if you're really hurting, we could put some dental cement on it, which we'd have to pick up from the drug store. Do you think that's necessary?" She gives me a look that says, "It's not really that serious, right?" and I shrug. It hurts, but there's no way I'm making her run out in her pajamas for something that isn't an actual emergency, according to the dentist.

"I'll be fine," I say, and she nods crisply, turning away from my eyes. Emergency Mom is folding herself up and filing herself away for next time, leaving me with Exhausted Mom, a less-stable model but we'll be okay as long as she doesn't morph into Martyr Mom, which is always a possibility when she's extra tired.

I take my aching mouth into my room and think about how to fill the hours.

THEN

(MEMORY JAR)

This doesn't count. This isn't a memory, but I have a feeling Celeste isn't going to take off points for not following the rubric, you know.

My face hurts like hell, and it's the smallest problem I have. I can't sit still—I don't have much room but I'm pacing, prowling like a lion even as I write. Scribble a line standing, walk to the closet door and pivot, massage my jaw. Prowl my way back, write another line.

Line lion line.

Sorry, no. This isn't a good space for poetry, and this isn't a good place to be alone. I can't leave, though, even if I could manage my pain and appear to be a normal human. Mom is sleeping but her mood is unstable. Dani is out with the cheer squad and I'm pacing with my phone open to the contacts screen, forcing myself to scroll past Scott's listing without dwelling on the panic and regret and the other hundred thousand feelings that cluster around that number.

I keep stopping at Joey's name, but what exactly am I going to say?

Okay, I have a memory for real. Something about Joey to put in this jar and never come out. I remember when it was just me and him, awake after that disaster of a spring break party Scott had while their parents went on that anniversary cruise.

"I'll wash, you dry?" said Joey, holding up two beer bottles in each hand. He was as drunk as anyone else, but somehow still on his feet and ready to clean.

"I'll hold the bag open," I said, bending down to get a garbage bag out of the cupboard under the sink. My head swam, and I had to sit on the floor for a minute. I traced the pattern on the linoleum with one finger. It was a curling filigree pattern, and I no longer cared about cleaning. Above me I could hear the tinny sound of music coming out of Joey's silly speakers built into the hood of his sweatshirt, which was loose against his back.

"Sorry about Jess," I said, thinking about how I should get up and cover Scott's legs with a blanket. They stuck up onto the arm of the couch that separated the dining room from the living room, his feet uncovered like always but so far away. "She wasn't good enough for you." I didn't know if that was true, but it was the right thing to say when a guy's date leaves the party with another guy. Jess was this waif of a girl with thick eye makeup and pink hair the shiny consistency of plastic. "You're lucky you're single, really," I went on, leaning my head against the cupboard to get a better view of Joey's face. "You still get to fall in love and feel all those fizzy feelings for the first time. That's still ahead of you."

Joey tipped back a glass of something clear sitting on the kitchen island. I hoped it was water. "I'm not meant to fall in love," he said, and the effort of shrugging was enough to make him stagger back a small step. "But hey, at least I'll have a smart, gorgeous sister-in-law, even if it's totally unfair that I didn't get to you before he did." He nodded toward Scott. "I'd be better than him, you know. I'd be better for you," he said, and I didn't answer, but I followed his gaze and focused all my attention on Scott's exposed feet.

There was too much silence then, but Joey passed out soon enough, and we pretended afterward that the conversation had either never happened or that neither of us remembered it, but I wonder if he still feels that way, and what it might mean that at times, like right now, I kind of wish that he did. Oh, hey, looks like I've got another page to burn.

NOW

I scroll past Joey's number and stop on Celeste. She told me to call. But again, what am I looking to say? I think about her making a call of her own, admitting me. Committing me. I imagine myself sitting in a rocking chair in a quiet room for a week or two. If I typed out the words, *I've thought about killing myself,* would she come running? Didn't I just decide to stop letting other people decide?

I've thought about killing myself. True enough, but I *didn't*. It doesn't seem like throwing myself into a mental hospital to avoid having to make a difficult decision should be the reason why I saved my own life. *Enough.* It has to be worth something, being alive, being in control of my brain. I scroll back to Scott's number and I can't help it, this time I dial, hold the phone up to my ear. I haven't tried to call him since the accident, so I'm unprepared to hear his voice, recorded a million years ago, a lifetime ago. "Hey, it's me, Scott. You can leave me a message if you want." *I want.* What do I want? The beep, and then I'm silent, barely a whisper of breath. I hang up. I feel full, too full of everything serious.

I'm dialing Joey before I can prepare myself, and when he answers all I can say is, "I hung up on his voicemail."

"I did too," he says.

"What if everything I thought about him was a lie?"

He doesn't answer, but the silence on the other end changes, like he's holding the phone away from his mouth, like he doesn't want me to hear.

"Hey," I say. "I chipped a tooth on a bottle of root beer and now I have to go to an emergency dentist appointment tomorrow, early."

He's back, a noise of empathy on the other side. "Oh, shit, Tay. That sucks."

"It really hurts." There's far too much whine in my voice.

"Do you want … " Joey trails off.

"What?"

"I don't know. I could come over. Keep you company?" His words tumble out, shy and apologetic, but I don't know. It sounds nice.

"I could sneak you in the bathroom window." It's Dani's preferred method of entry in the summer, but Scott's climbed through in the winter before. The hallway makes a nice L shape right before my mom's room, and the bathroom window is hidden from her window by this enormous cedar shrub. She might see the footprints, if she cared to wade through the snow around the side of the house, which is unlikely to begin with, but even so, she'd probably assume they were Dani's.

This is a bad idea, probably. Or even a stupid one, I don't know. It doesn't seem to matter when everything hurts.

Ten minutes later my phone buzzes and I direct him to the wall outside my bathroom window. I slip down the attic stairs in my socks, checking to make sure my mom is still in her room. All's clear, so I help him climb in the window, lithe like a little cat. He makes almost no sound until we're safely up in my room with the door closed.

"That was sort of exciting," he says, and he sits on the end of my bed without seeming to focus on the fact that he's sitting on his comatose brother's girlfriend's *bed*. "Are you going to tell the dentist about the baby?"

"It crosses the placental barrier," I say, my hand clamped over my mouth. I still haven't looked in the mirror.

He nods. "Probably better tell, then." He pats the bed next to him, and I sit. "Can I see the new wound, Scarface?"

I smile, but I keep my hand up over my mouth until he wrestles it out of the way, or at least he tries, but I'm laughing and pushing him away and then nothing is funny and his fingers are gripping my wrist so I can feel his pulse and he can feel mine, and we're both breathing hard and I'm suddenly certain he's going to kiss me, and I know it's shock and grief and all kinds of other stupid things. But I've pretty much decided I'm going to kiss him back, and that's better than jumping off a cliff, you know?

My hand drops and my mouth falls opens a little. He

sees my tooth and pulls back in dismay. He drops his hands from my wrists. "That looks like it hurts."

I turn away, my face hot. "I miss him," I say. It's as good an explanation as anything for whatever just happened, for what might happen later. For everything.

Joey gently takes off my glasses and sets them on my bedside table. "Close your eyes," he says, and his fingers dig into my scalp in a way that actually pulls my attention away from the pain in my jaw for a second. They climb up to the crown of my head like expert mountaineers, then trail lightly down to the nape of my neck and settle in a base camp there, loosening the muscles of my neck.

"Emily swears he said my name," says Joey. "I wasn't in the room, but Emily was reading to him. Some dumb thing from a cooking magazine, probably, I didn't ask. I didn't want to know." He pushes his thumbs into the space between my shoulders and everything inside me collapses. "But, you know, anything can sound like Joe."

I slump over until I'm lying on my side, my head at the foot of my bed. I can barely listen to his voice; his hands are all that exists. No baby, no brother, no boyfriend, no brain injury. No bottle, no broken tooth. I feel my consciousness start to slide off of me, like a heavy blanket in the middle of the night. "Joe." I don't have anything else to say.

"I don't believe Emily," Joey says, his hands falling still on my back. "He's not going to wake up and be normal." He speaks so softly I almost don't believe that I hear him. "But I want you to know I've made a decision, Taylor. I'm here for you and this baby, no matter what happens with my brother."

Everybody's making decisions for me and this baby. I curl my body slightly away from him, and all I want to do is pretend that I didn't hear. "You fixed it," I say. I make my voice thick and sleepy.

"Shhh," says Joey, pulling a patchwork quilt that my grandma made over me. "You go ahead and tell them in the morning, Tay. Tell the dentist, not your mom."

"Okay." I agree with a meaningless word and then I'm floating, no thoughts for whether Joey will be there when I wake up or no.

THEN

(MEMORY JAR)

I dreamed you tried to read my mind
that in fact you claimed complete legal ownership to all
my insides via some complex copyright tangle that I had once
agreed to with a glance or breath or something spoken
all in some other tongue—
witnessed by nothing
and judged

I dreamed I called you up
and swore at you
and asked you to sit beside me
thread your fingers in my hair
and worry but when I unclose
uncurl
undream—

you are quite gone.

NOW

My phone buzzes, wakes me at three a.m., the blue light flashing on and off. It's Dani, texting the second she got home.

You need anything? I'm home now. Saw that stupid mess online. You know I would kill someone before telling your secrets, right?

My room is pitch black and I'm facing the wrong way, my head all thick with an aching pain and memory—I reach my hand out, looking for Joey, for Scott, for anyone. I switch on the desk lamp, blinking away the brightness, fumbling with the dimmer. Nobody is here. I pull on my glasses and text back. The mess online. My mouth.

I'm good now but chipped my tooth at pizza. Dentist tomorrow.

It's not like I expected him to stay with me. That would be weird, right? This whole thing is weird. I do a mental status update—do I feel pregnant? The thing Joey said, right before I fell asleep. Did he really say it? See? Completely weird. My bladder is screaming at me, and my scar itches, but there's no nausea and there's no other reminder that my life is situated along a fault line that is rapidly sliding toward destruction. I wrap my patchwork quilt around me and tiptoe downstairs to the bathroom, checking to see that Joey closed the window all the way. It's weird to think of Joey here, in my bathroom, where I'm peeing. The thought of him escaping alone, leaving me asleep on my bed where he'd touched me. My chest feels strangely tight, the air in the house too thick for comfort.

You chipped your tooth???!!!?!?!?!!!

A giggle escapes. This is why I need Dani. I should have texted her hours ago, cheer squad be damned. I know she needs to have some time away from my drama, but the fact remains that it's three in the morning and I'm in pain and in crisis, and her fourteen separate bits of alarmed end punctuation are the one thing guaranteed to make me feel an intense relief.

It will be okay. I pause, thinking for a moment too long about Joey calling me Scarface, about the moment I might have let him kiss me.

She sends me back a string of emojis that make me know I'm loved, and then a little sleepy panda that lets me know she's going to bed, and I fall back on my pillow and allow myself to go to sleep, hoping for no more dreams, no more poetry.

THEN

(MEMORY JAR)

I had another stupid dream, but this time when I woke up there was something I could remember, something I could write here and really mean it. In the dream I was sitting beside Scott in some indeterminate place, like a bus station or maybe an actual bus, I don't know. We were sitting next to each other and looking straight ahead, and I held on to the side of his arm but he didn't act like he noticed. We didn't talk at all for some time, but there did seem to be movement, and gradually I became aware of this sound, a sort of humming crescendo. It was a mechanical sound, which is where my mind maybe got the idea of a bus from, but it didn't sound right. It was high-pitched and too steady—too steadily *increasing*, actually.

"It's wrong," I said, and I pulled at Scott's arm, but the

skin of his hand pulled off like the little flappy armchair covers, the kind that grandmas have crocheted on the arms of all their chairs, and stuffing came pouring out of the hole. "Oh, shit," I said, in the dream, and I think the shock of swearing out loud is what woke me, looking around in the dream world to see who might have heard. Funny that the shocking thing was a stupid word and not the fact that my boyfriend's arm was apparently a pillow that was tearing apart beneath my fingers or that there was this deadly crescendo of sound ringing in my ears.

That sound. That's what I remember. It was wrong, the tone of it and the steady build. It was an engine sound, and there was something wrong, and I remember a kind of panicked pulling, too, and the urgent thought, *slow down*. I remember that, but then it gets all fuzzy with pillow-arms and disintegrating and then we're back to various blood-red puddles in the snow, only some of them real.

NOW

Mom is overly worried about the condition of my face, given the circumstances. "It hurts to the touch," I say, but she's insistent and dab-dab-dabs at my sore face with a wet cotton ball. I can't tell if she's wiping off new blood or trying to scrub off the scabs from the accident.

"Doctor Zimmerman is seeing you on a Saturday as a personal favor," she says, and I don't understand.

"You know the dentist?" Mom's had a half cup of coffee and is somewhat anxious, but not super irritable, this morning, so I don't mind pushing her a little. I think about what Joey said, about telling Dr. Z but not telling Mom. The hospital privacy policy had been pretty specific about the things they were required to reveal to a parent/guardian, and I imagine the dental contract couldn't be that different. But will Mom's friend tell her, as a personal favor?

"There's more to it than that," says my mom, after a pause. She pulls away from my face at last and tosses the cloth across the spout of the sink. "We're sort of behind on our insurance."

"I thought we were good until March." I know getting us insured after the office closes is something my mom's been stressing about, but it's only January.

"Well." She sighs, and the weight of this shows. "My employer seems to have dropped the ball on meeting our premiums, and, well, they're going bankrupt anyway, so they haven't been all that concerned with this."

"What about our health insurance? What about the bills from the crash?"

She stands up and finishes the second half of her coffee in one long swig. "No need to worry about what we can't control," she says. "Some of it depends on the insurance investigation, what they determine to be the cause of the crash, but probably all the hospital bills will get paid by Scott's parents' insurance."

Probably, depending on the investigation? What does that mean, even? Is there an outcome that would make us liable? "We can't handle all those medical bills." I offer this thought as though it's something that won't have occurred to her. "Didn't the insurance company tell you this was happening before we got dropped?"

"Look, Taylor. Just rinse your mouth out carefully one more time, and we'll take care of this dental thing." She bends over to toss the cotton balls into the garbage can. "They sent us a note, but I didn't read it or understand it very well. I was stressed, and there's so much piling up all the time." She takes a quick breath, and I can tell we're done talking about this—about anything—for the time being. "It doesn't matter. Doctor Z and I will work it out as soon as I've got coverage again."

The dentist is a friend of my mom's. She's totally going to make sure my mom finds out if I tell her I'm pregnant, even if the privacy policy says she can't. I know, I should tell her. Last night, it might have worked. This morning, maybe before she brought up the insurance thing, but now? No. Maybe after my therapy appointment this afternoon. Maybe I can practice by telling Celeste.

The dentist looks remarkably put together for an early, unexpected Saturday, but she doesn't smile much all the same. There's no receptionist and no assistant, and Dr. Zimmerman searches through three places before she finds the patient consent and privacy form. I watch my mom's pen skip across the boxes, checking *no, no, no*. No heart disease. No current medications. No autoimmune disorder. I watch her fill out my height (correct) and weight (um, yeah, when I was twelve, Mom). No history of allergies. No alcohol or drug abuse. She doesn't even pause as she checks the *no* box for the question of pregnant or nursing, doesn't even look up. In her head I *am* twelve, and she carefully records the date of my recent concussion and an explanation of the accident.

"Thanks, Jen," Doctor Zimmerman says, smiling at my mom and glancing at the page quickly before tucking it into the clipboard and ushering me into the exam room. "I'll stop out once I have an idea how long it will be."

"We really appreciate this," says my mom, sinking into a chair in the waiting room.

"Let's take a look-see, Taylor," says Doctor Zimmerman, and then she nods toward the clipboard. "That was quite a crash you were in, wasn't it. I read about it in the newspaper, saw there was an update site for the boy. How's he doing? Was he your boyfriend?"

"He is, actually," I say, but then she's got all this crap in my mouth and I can't really tell her anything.

THEN

There were things I didn't tell him, even that actual night, like the breaking up part. But the idea that there could be another girl, that it could be this ponytail-swinging Kendall person telling me they had a "relationship," that he'd made such a bizarre promise? Even though it can't be true, I'm pissed that he left me alone with nothing but my memory to deal with all of this crap. The only thing is, I'm not really sure how to be pissed at him, right now.

So I'm thinking about keeping secrets, and I'm thinking in particular about hiding your friendship (or whatever) with another person, especially a female person, from your girlfriend, even your "back home in high school" girlfriend, and I'm thinking that's worse than neglecting—or delaying—to tell your mom (and your dentist) that you're pregnant. It's lying, you know, the slippery kind of lying that involves leaving out all the relevant details. He never once talked about Kendall's hard times, or Kendall's sister with cancer. There was no hint of her, other than one brief introduction and those few whiffs of soap. I was about to break up with him, but was it all distance, or was some of it his disinterest? Worse, did it go so far as secrecy and lies? Was he actually cheating on me with her? And even if they weren't hooking up, did he go to her for emotional support instead of me? Did he confide in her, complain about me? How much of my business was he sharing with this other person? Did he tell her I almost jumped off "a bridge or something," and if so, why are the facts just a little bit off? If he was going to let her have the baby (as if he had the right to do that), why did he ask me to marry him? None of it is right, and my brain worries the issue like a puppy gnawing on a rawhide. So if I could talk to Doctor Zimmerman and answer her question properly, here is what I would say about *how the boy is doing*:

The boy is lying. He's lying in a bed in a hospital and he won't tell me what the hell is going on or what I should do or what this all is or anything. He's got some kind of secret life he didn't tell me anything about, and I'm having his baby. I almost broke up with him, and I have his engagement ring sealed in a little cellophane packet in the pocket of my hoodie. His little brother has decided to be my noble savior or something and, equally strange, I'm finding myself sort of attracted to that idea even as I'm repulsed by how messed up it is. Also, my boyfriend's in a coma, and nobody really seems like they have any idea when or if he'll ever wake up.

NOW

When I enter Scott's room, Kendall jumps up like someone guilty of a crime, one hand raised in a kind of greeting or a kind of surrender. "I'm so sorry," she says. "I couldn't leave things like they were."

"What are you even doing here?" I can't believe she came back. I can't focus on this right now. The world feels less real with my mouth all numb and puffy from the anesthesia I wasn't supposed to use—*"crosses the placental barrier"*—and my mom arranged for me to see Celeste in like twenty minutes even though it's Saturday, and here is this girl, coming at me with her mouth running about things I don't want any part of.

"I know it was hard for you to hear about the adoption idea from me," she begins, and I hold my hand up.

"Kendall, stop—" Nobody needs to remind me that this whole situation is ill-advised at best. Instant vacation to anywhere else right now, preferably somewhere without any connections to anyone else in my life. I don't feel pregnant at this moment. Does this conversation, this emotion, this *feeling* have an impact on the kid-thing's brain? Does awkwardness cross the placental barrier? Does distraction? Am I giving my future kid ADHD right now by having numbing medicine at the dentist without telling her I'm pregnant and by looking at Kendall right now and actually, vividly, *wanting* to kill her? Can your mother's murderous impulse screw you up in utero?

"Taylor!" Emily rushes into the room, a burst of apology. "She just showed up!"

"Listen," says Kendall, ignoring Emily's fluttering protests. "I know we only met that once, at the game, but I tried to get him to let you down easy. He was sweet on you, of course. There was a lot of fondness there, but I told him he shouldn't lead you on anymore. I couldn't see him throwing away his future for you, for a *marriage* that wouldn't last."

"A marriage?" says Emily, perking up. Her face is so hopeful, so confused. So fucking sad, like all of us, all the time.

"I wanted him to be happy," says Kendall.

I hold her gaze. "But not with me." Happiness. Is this a thing we're going to talk about right now? I wouldn't *really* murder her, you know. But what does she mean when she claims they talked about me all the time? What did he tell her about me? And why didn't he tell *me* about her?

"He loved me," says Kendall.

"I think you might actually be crazy," I say, and I want Scott to wake up, right this instant. I want him to sit up and see me, the set of my chin as I face her. I want him to sit up straight with that lazy smile of his, and he'll remember everything, and his first word will be "Sweetness," and Kendall will swing her athletic ponytail out of our lives, and we will show her what happiness looks like.

Well, I may only be the high school girlfriend, but I have a pretty good idea that happiness is some kind of irrational-number emotion. I mean, I don't know what I'm talking about mathematically—my calc tutor would surely tell you about my abysmal understanding of numerical concepts—but even though I don't always know what every theorem or whatever is called, I still feel like I understand some things about math, especially the parts that are sort of like poetry. Anyway, I think happiness is like the math problem where there's a point, you know? And you're always approaching it without ever arriving, always managing to split the distance in half, but you're still only halfway there. And maybe that's okay. Maybe there's a value in stopping, you know? In getting close enough.

"Please," says Kendall. "Let me explain."

As far as I'm concerned, she's explained enough, but clearly she's not going anywhere without saying her piece. Emily squeezes my hand. "I'll be right out in the hall if you need me," she promises.

THEN

(KENDALL)

I only want to explain. I met Scott at the practice arena. I play on the women's hockey team, and Scott refereed at a few of our scrimmages. My roommate was in his sociology class, and my other roommate was his comp instructor. We were kind of on the edges of each other's circles. We talked a few times, only a few minutes here and there, standing in skates, you know, but we kept running into each other. On campus, all over. We had coffee a few times, studied together. As friends, I swear. He was easy to talk to, okay? And it was so … it was just random, but we had a lot in common.

There's more than I've told you, okay? More about my family, my sister's cancer, all of that, but also more about me. He was a good listener, okay? That's all. I talked, and he listened, at a time when I really needed someone to listen.

Maybe you can't understand. I know you never wanted this baby, but my sister—she was born to be a mom. She raised me and my younger brother after our own mother died, also cancer. Stupid cancer. She had a miscarriage once, like five years ago, and it broke her, okay? Being a mother, caring for babies, it's what she was made for. Every month when she didn't get pregnant, I could see more and more of her slipping away, and I couldn't stand to see her despairing. When the cancer came—it was so cruel. She was so strong.

This is where my plan came in, okay? I just want you to understand. Okay, so this is the part. Hear me out? I decided to try to get pregnant for her—like, she would adopt and I could be the baby's aunt? And Scott, well, I asked him if he would . . . no, Taylor, wait. Oh my god, this is so random. I'm blushing. But wait. He was supposed to talk with you about this, months ago, but then you came down and you told him about the baby and, well, we thought it was the perfect solution, okay?

I'd do anything for my sister, but you know. Being pregnant, I'd have to give up hockey and probably my whole scholarship. I mean, even though this was a choice I was making out of love for my sister and wanting to give her something she couldn't have for herself, it wasn't easy. And Scott understood. The hockey thing especially, okay?

Taylor, when he found out about the baby—when you came down and told him you were pregnant—*oh, by the way, never mind that I've known for a few weeks already and I've decided to get an abortion, la-dee-dah*—when that happened, and then when you sped back up north to your little high school friends, who do you think he called? Who do you think was there for him?

The only stupid idea he had for convincing you not to do it was to ask you to marry him. He came to my apartment that night, I guess right after you left. He was crying. He wasn't even there, do you know what I mean? Like his eyes were open but his mind was missing. I mean I know that sounds awful, given what's going on now, but I hadn't ever seen him like that. I know it's awful, and I mean nothing against you, but you're in *high school*, for god's sake. I told him no, marrying you was not the solution. The real solution was so simple, and it would make everyone happy. You say I don't know what would make him happy, but he liked my idea. It's what Scott would have wanted.

NOW

"Scott wasn't a good listener." I didn't even say the word abortion until the night of the crash, and even then I only said it once, and I'm not sure if he heard me. I swear, it was the first time I'd ever said the word out loud. I rack my brain, but there's nothing to this story. "He only looked like he was listening while he was waiting to kiss you."

I can't believe what she's telling me, that Scott spent the night at her apartment crying about me, promising our potential baby to her sister. That before that, Scott was going to ... help *her* get pregnant? No. I can't believe any of this. I sit back down on the chair beside Scott's bed. I want him to wake up. Enough, already, enough of this wait-ing. I don't understand. When he said those words, when he did that throat-clearing business, everyone acted so happy, like for sure it was only a moment or two away, and Scott was going to wake up and either it would all be the same or … not. I thought he'd be back by now. "Look. I didn't go down there all *la-dee-dah*, okay?" I imitate her stupid up-talking verbal tic. "You're right. I'm *in high school*. And I had to hurry back because my mom didn't allow me to drive all the way down to St. Cloud alone. I didn't know about this for weeks and weeks before telling him—I hadn't told him because, what, was I going to text him about it? I'm only seventeen years old, you know. It's kind of a big deal to find out that your whole life—all your planning for the future and double-majoring and being good at something—all of that has to change because you're fucking pregnant."

The face she makes, the look on Kendall's face as she stares behind me, lets me know instantly that someone has been standing behind me listening, hearing everything I've just said, but I can't tell, without turning around, who it is. Is it Emily, standing guard in the hall? Is it my mom, overhearing what I've been too afraid to tell her? Is it Scott's mom, in so much pain already that she's been taking meds to help her cope? There are so many weights hanging from any of those possibilities, my chest is crushed completely. "Who is it?" I can't turn around.

"I have no clue," says Kendall, which means probably not any of my guesses. I turn. It's Celeste, and Lydia, the nurse from the ICU.

"I helped her find you over here in the rehab unit," Lydia says, and she steps back into the hallway. She doesn't say a word beyond the necessary, but her eyes tell me that she's made for compassion, for healing people. It's something I'm happy to get a chance to see.

"Your session starts now," says Celeste. "Or actually a few minutes ago."

"Perfect timing," I say, and then I walk by her side to the office with walls that go all the way up to the ceiling. And glue guns.

THEN

(TO CELESTE)

In *my* memory of things, there was a brief hug, a dazed look, the sort of physically visible bottling-up. If he was so sad, if he cried so hard in *Kendall's* apartment, why couldn't he spare any emotion for me? Why didn't he say anything about the possibilities, about what he was worried about, any of that? Why did he barely text me all that evening—seriously, I even forwarded the few terse, one-word responses he'd sent me on to Dani so the two of us could dissect them. Thinking about him going to Kendall for comfort makes me queasy, that there was someone in his life he shared more with than he shared with me. And seriously, did he promise my *baby* to her, like my child is some kind of commodity that he can trade? No. Everything about this story unravels for me there.

I remember driving back up north in a fog, unable to cry. I remember that awful feeling like I was too full of everything. I remember distracting myself from it all in the library with Dani, and I remember holding my hands over my belly in the night feeling all that weight settle down on me. I remember sitting up in the center of my bed with my headphones on but no music playing, just a terrible idea running through my mind.

NOW

No. Not talking anymore. Not ending up on the fourth floor.

Celeste tries to act like everything is normal, but I can tell she's on edge by the way she sits on her specially ordered, comfy, lily-pad therapy chair—she's stiff and poised to spring. To leap into action, to solve this problem. Me.

"It must be so shocking finding out that Scott had secrets, things you didn't know about his life at college," she says, and even the way she bends her elbows is anxious for me to speak, to spill.

"It's not the secrets," I say, and she leans in. "It's everything all at once."

"Have you told your mother?" she asks, her voice gentle. I shake my head very slightly. No. I have not told my mother.

"Do you want to talk about Kendall?"

"I sort of want Kendall to not exist for a while," I say,

and it's the kind of thing I like the sound of, so I say it in my head again. I don't want to kill her; I'm not unhinged in that kind of awful way. But I do want to be able to sit by my boyfriend and talk to him without seeing her there, telling her own versions of things that don't even make sense.

"Do you want to talk about Scott's recovery?" she says, and I swear she pulls out this clump of purple clay or something, and she divides this big lump into two pieces and hands one to me across the table. I mean, she doesn't plunk it on the table near me—she holds it out in front of her, the whole weight of it making her arm go a bit shaky before I finally realize I'm going to have to reach out and actually take the horrid thing in my hand, or she's going to have to decide to set it down, and it's this whole battle of the wills, and then my fingernails are sinking into the clay and I'm squishing the whole works into a ball in the palm of my hand. We both sit there, kneading the clay for a while, Celeste with her giant fingernails and everything all caked in purple clay.

"It's not much of a recovery," I say, giving the clay a good pinch. In the beginning, the waiting was acute—we were hoping he would make it through the night, we were waiting to see if his brain would stop swelling in time, waiting for him to breathe on his own. "I thought he was making progress, but then he stopped." It's hard to face the idea that this may be as good as it gets. That the miraculous, feel-good ending is not always the ending you get—that in fact you may not get an ending so much as a really sad beginning.

"It's hard to keep a positive attitude about progress some-times," says Celeste, and she says it in a way that makes it feel like an observation of the world, not a comment about me. She pinches her own pile of clay, and I wonder how much of this talking through trauma with other people might help her in thinking about her own stuff. For a moment it makes me want to be a therapist, too. A cardiologist, a poet, and a ther-apist, all at once. There are so many paths and possibilities, but this queasy pit in my middle could cut them all short.

"You're really good at empathy," I tell her, and I peel off a small chunk of purple clay and start to roll it in my hands, warming it into a soft, moldable body. "I'm sure this would be hard without any added complications, you know?" This is safe. I'm not coming off as suicidal or worse. And really, what's the harm now, right? If this is my life, if this continues to be my life, I guess I'll need to get used to people knowing about it and talking about it. The clay baby sits cradled in my palm.

"He might get better, and he might not," says Celeste. "And either option might take a lot more time than you've thought about, than you've imagined."

I can't crush the little purple baby blob, so I take the rest of the clay and gently mold it all around the smaller piece, smoothing out the edges with my fingertips. "I'm sort of alone in this, no matter how many people know," I say, and Celeste doesn't answer but she reaches over and pats my clay thing, which I've molded into an imprint of the space inside my clasped hands. I put it down on the table, and I pick up my memory jar. "I think I've got another story to go in," I say.

THEN

(TO CELESTE)

Scott took the news, like I told Dani, stoic and whatever. He was reassuring but stiff, and there was that smell on his shirt when he hugged me. I know it was a surprise, and maybe boys don't actually understand that just because I was six weeks pregnant, it didn't mean that I'd *known about this for six weeks*. I told him as soon as I could. I had no idea it was bothering him, the fact that I hadn't told him immediately. I mean, I was working things through with Dani. She's my best friend, and she was there, in my room, on my phone, beside my locker. She kept the secret from everyone else, and she helped me plan out how to tell him. I don't know what I expected when I drove down to St. Cloud all the way from Sterling Creek, skipping my afternoon classes and risking my mom's wrath, but I kind of expected more than a stiff hug and a stiff upper lip. And I swear I didn't say anything about getting an abortion. I couldn't have, because honestly, I hadn't thought that far until after I saw his reaction. This part of Kendall's story is false. How much of the rest is, too? Uncertainty rises up, this feeling that I should have known, and at the same time that I shouldn't have trusted him. But what if he's innocent? What if this Kendall person is lying to me?

When I told him I was pregnant, there was a super childish part of me that thought he'd fix everything, that his response would tell me exactly what I needed to do about everything. I mean, maybe I even dreamed that he would ask me to marry him then, or at the very least promise, like his brother has, to be there for me and for our baby through it all. Instead, I got nothing, or at least nothing reassuring.

So whose story is true? Whose memory is false? I want him to wake up and tell me if he really has changed so much, hidden so much from me. If he doesn't wake up, how will I ever know the truth?

NOW

Joey's there when I walk out of Celeste's office, several minutes over time, but Celeste asked me to read my memory out loud to her and then print it for the memory jar. She said it's important to get my feelings down in a way that I can hold in my hands, that I can crumple up or seal into the jar or burn to cinders when I'm done holding on to them.

"Hey," he says. He shrugs beneath his canvas mechanic jacket. "Can I see the new smile?"

"What?" I've almost forgotten about the stupid tooth, but I get it, a second late, and somehow him catching me off-guard like that makes me actually smile, and he nods.

"It looks good, honest."

"I didn't tell them," I say, shaking my head. "I had the numbing medicine."

"Gas?" His eyebrows draw together a little, like he's worrying.

"No gas. I told her it makes me dizzy."

"It's probably okay." He tips his chin toward Scott's room. "Tay. I've been talking to Tom, you know, the guy from the news?" He waits for me to nod. "So he started thinking about the story of Kendall, you know. Her sister's uterine cancer, her plans to carry a child for her sister, the comatose sperm donor?"

"I suppose there's a story there, though I don't want any part of it."

"You want a part of this, believe me. It's kind of incredible."

"Yeah?" I still haven't had any answer from Scott's roommates, no evidence that any of what Kendall says is really true. "Incredible how?"

Joey leans in closer. "So Tom did some research and found out that Kendall doesn't *have* a sister. The whole story's bunk."

"She's *lying*?" My voice rises to a squeak, and I force it back down to a low whisper, but *come on*. "She couldn't have lied about that forever. There would've been adoption paperwork. I mean, she doesn't think I'd just hand over this baby in a wicker basket, right? Does she think nobody would look into those facts?" Is she legitimately insane? How far would she let this charade go on? My phone buzzes, and I'm unprepared for what I see. "Oh, god." The words escape from my mouth and I almost puke. The picture shows an aborted fetus, chopped up into pieces. I close my eyes and sway on my feet.

"What is it?" says Joey. "Should we step outside for a quick fresh air break?" The concern in his voice is real. He puts an arm out to steady me, and I show him the awful picture. I let him take my arm. "Oh, fuck. What . . ." He scrolls through the other messages, from the other numbers. "Are these all from her?" His face is pale and he hands the phone back to me.

"I thought they were spam at first." I can't help seeing the image one more time when I close the message and switch over to the text from my mom, which tells me to catch a ride home from Joey if I can. "I might throw up."

I'm shaky and sick, and I lean on his arm as we head to the elevator, taking deep breaths. Saliva pools in my mouth, and I'm tired of this, you know? It's downright exhausting to be nauseated all the time, and it feels unfair that I have to deal with all this without Scott, and I want to curl up in the corner of the elevator and weep, but Joey holds me up.

"Easy, Tay," he murmurs. A smoke break is one of those dependable ways to make sure time is passing even in the hospital, where all time is stretched out into endless waiting—so Joey and I have been taking fresh-air breaks instead. It's not much like taking a smoke break, honestly, but at this moment it's a welcome change from the close personal atmosphere of Celeste's office before heading into the strangely heavy but impersonal air of Scott's room, and it definitely beats the anxious cloud that settles into the family waiting area. I'm steady on my feet by the time we go through the main doors, even if I look ridiculous sucking oxygen into my lungs and spitting all my extra saliva into the snowbank by the sidewalk. Instead of heading right or left along the sidewalk, or just hanging around the door like we usually do, we cross the street wordlessly and stare into the gated cemetery. I'm not sure what Joey's thinking as we look through the gates—maybe he's worried about his brother ending up under all that frozen earth—but all I can see is Kendall, who apparently made up that entire story about the cancer and carrying a baby to give up for adoption, and what does that mean about Scott? What does that mean about this "relationship" they allegedly had? Is everything a lie?

"Do you think she's dangerous?" I blow my breath vapor through the gate like I'm really smoking. We've called the latest number back and let it ring a million times.

"I'm going to find out everything, every bit of dirt I can get on that girl," says Joey. He slams his fist against the iron bars, making me jump back beneath the rattle. "What the hell, Taylor? Why didn't you tell me someone was sending you shit like that? She's fucking lucky she's not still here. And I'm going to make damn sure she's not allowed to show up here again." He hits the gate again, and it scares me a little at the same time as it thrills me. I'm not entirely alone. Joey is on my side.

THEN

(MEMORY JAR)

Joey drove me to Dani's house from the hospital this afternoon since there wasn't another bus coming for almost two hours, and while we were waiting for the car to warm up in the parking lot, he asked me if I'm thinking about the past too much. He wondered if I was afraid of the future.

This only happened like five minutes ago, but it was five minutes that I wouldn't mind remembering, so I'm writing it down. I don't know why people say we should "live in the moment." I feel like we're all living in one eternally awful moment that never comes to an end. But sometimes there are good things in the middle of all this pain, moments I don't mind living, and the ride home with Joey today was one of them. Also this moment right now, writing in Dani's tree fort bed, snuggling with a bunch of stuffed spiders.

NOW

"Instant Vacation," says Dani, but she doesn't say where. She takes a long look at me and pushes Neep into my face. His eight fuzzy legs dangle into my ears and hair, and I can feel the worn spot where little Dani rubbed her thumb against his little spider tummy, all those years ago when she cuddled him in the orphanage.

"Well, this isn't much of a vacay," I say, blowing fluffy spider fur out of my mouth.

"I don't know where to take you," she says. "I don't know how to fix this."

I turn my head, letting Neep slip off my face. "What if your mom had had an abortion?" I ask. The question is hollow and far away, and I know it might hurt her, but this is where we are, this vacation.

She's quiet—not so quiet I suspect I've crossed a line, but

quiet enough that I know she's taking my question seriously. I think Dani's adoption is something so much a part of her and her moms' personal narratives—the whole blogging adventure, complete with photos—and so much a part of who she is to me that I guess I don't realize that being adopted means she's part of a group of other people with their own adoption stories. I should have been thinking about how all of this might be hurting her, on a different level.

"Are you asking, because I'm adopted, how do I feel about abortion?" Dani takes a little breath, a hitch that I can hear, and then she lets it out in a little puff. "I guess I think … I think there are spirits of people who are waiting to be born, and I would have jumped the next ship. I'm not too attached to my genetic material, really, and I think it's sort of luck of the draw where each person ends up, physically."

"Like karma luck, or just random?"

Another little sigh. "I'd *like* it better if it were karma luck," she says.

I hug my arms around my body. "Me too," I say, and then I think for a while. "Maybe."

THEN

(TO DANI)

I remember one time I asked my mom why she hadn't given me up for adoption if I was such a pain in the ass and turned her life to shit like she said. It must have been one of those times where there was no stopping the collision, where we were both so far over the line that it didn't matter one way or the other what I said or did, I was still screwed. Sometimes I kind of liked those times because I knew where I stood, anyway, and I could speak my mind.

"I loved your father, and he loved me," was all she said.

"Why did he leave?" Everything about me was a challenge, from the set of my mouth to my firmly planted feet. "If you guys were so in love, why did he leave?"

Kids can be such little shits, you know? There's this strange tide turning within me, and I keep on seeing things from her point of view. I keep seeing my mom's vulnerability, her struggle. It's not much fun to see adults as humans—as people with the same issues we have—instead of heroes or villains. It means getting way too close to being grown-up.

How easy it would have been for her to spit out at me what is probably the truth—*he left because of you.*

NOW

Dani holds the spider, cradling him in her arms in a way that is habitual and a little heartbreaking. "I don't think your mom is messing you up, Tay," she says in a soft voice. "I think you're both good people doing your best."

I peer out of the leafy canopy at the room, which is pure Dani. On the walls, a muted palette: grass-mat texture, a mural of an endless savannah. A solitary lion on the horizon, with the sense of others behind it. Dani's moms had found it enchanting and humorously ironic when Dani requested they design her room after the Ray Bradbury short story where the kids have their holographic nursery lions eat their parents. Janie wrote a whole series of posts on her blog about it and the whole thing made them get several requests for bedroom redesigns. They made a little extra cash off that idea and spent a week in Mexico together, the three of them, and they asked me to go along. My mom wouldn't allow me to go, and anyway, I had no passport, no spending money. It would have been strange to have gone. But oh, I wanted to.

"I won't ever get to travel," I say. "I won't ever get to see the whole world."

"Or," she says, "you might discover the world with your kid."

"On my earnings as a poet?"

She laughs. "Well, let's not get carried away. Maybe your cardiologist income will have to take care of some of the travel expenses. The poetry could buy you, maybe, a really cute handbag."

"And for my kid? What do I get for him?"

Dani thinks for a moment, then smiles. "Your kid will need a really professional camera. He's going to take glamorous photographs of you for his art class that will someday show up in a fancy magazine, like fancy people buy from a fancy art shop and then put them on display. Fancily." She starts to giggle.

"A *fahncy* coffee table book," I say, and I'm laughing, too. "Dahling."

"After that, it's only a matter of time before you're publishing your memoir, what's it called again?"

I think too long, wondering how to sum up my life. "*This Memoir is Fiction?*"

"No, no, that's not sappy enough. We'll call it *To Mend a Broken Heart*," she says. "And obviously the play on words with the heart surgeon piece, yeah?"

I roll my eyes.

"*A Song of Heart Mending*," she goes on, barely able to get the words out between giggles. "*Doctor Heart's Mending Song.*"

"Oh my god, Dani, stop. My stomach—" I can't breathe from laughing ridiculously. "Probably more accurate if my title mentioned a broken head," I say, and the words pull all the fizz out of our moment. It gets quiet again, in our little tree fort in the murderous veldt. "I can't really have a baby, Dani."

"This isn't fair, you know, any of this." She takes my hand and squeezes it, and I don't know what to do anymore, so I don't do anything. Fair is irrelevant.

THEN

(DANI)

I remember when you bought those matching sweatshirts. You know, the ones from St. Cloud State? You got them for some special event in your relationship, like your twenty-two-month kiss-iversary or something revolting like that, and you were wearing them at this party. It was out at that Cody guy's place, and they had a bonfire, and there were like thirty people there I didn't know and you guys, a matched pair. No, I'm not saying there was anything wrong with it, Taylor. I mean, the two of you were always reaching for each other, and the best part was that neither one of you was reaching more often than the other, I remember that.

There was nothing wrong with the two of you, but there was something—I can't even explain it. At the time I dismissed it as my own jealousy because, you know, I was there with some mouth-breather off the hockey team who, between you and Cody, I somehow got matched up with. He wasn't a mouth-breather, that isn't fair. It was Jason Adams, actually, and he had nice hair and pretty eyes even if he wasn't much for, I don't know, conversations that involved ideas or curiosity. That's what it was! Between you and Scott. A lack of curiosity. You know how, when you first meet someone, you want to know everything about them? You want to know what they're doing every single minute, and you want to think about how cute they are when they're doing those things? You and Scott ... that night, around the fire, you were there, in each other's sweatshirts, but I didn't see you thinking about each other's lives, outside of that night. Do you hear what I'm saying? You were his girlfriend, and he was your boyfriend, and that was an accepted fact, but neither of you had the look of a person *in love*. A person who is always thinking, always wondering about the other person.

NOW

I swear, we did not call it a kiss-iversary. He bought the sweatshirts, actually, and I was angry at him that night, something to do with the whole party thing, and he and Cody forcing me to drag Dani along by setting her up with one of their friends. I didn't want to spend our one evening together at some stupid bonfire party surrounded by all of his friends, is that so terrible?

"Oh god," I say. "It's my fault."

"What are you talking about?" Dani shifts beside me, tries to get a good look at me, but I cover my face with my hands.

"You're right. I'm so stupid. I wasn't interested in knowing his friends, in seeing his life or who he was becoming." The realization makes me sick to my stomach. I wanted *our* lives to continue on, in stasis, until I could graduate and join him somewhere down the line. I wanted to seal him under a bubble and keep him "my boyfriend" without anything changing, trapped inside our little high school romance. I'm such an idiot.

"It's natural, though, don't you think?" Dani pulls my hands down and tries to pin me down with her dark eyes. "The two of you were mismatched from the start."

Natural. I can see what she means, and I know the difference between us would never have been that big of a deal if we'd met later, if we'd both been in college or all the way grown up. I think about how unfathomable Scott's high school life was to ninth grade me, visiting him in the weight room after school, and I wonder if I've always been wrong for him, like Dani's saying. Like he said plenty of times in the beginning too, I guess. That sounds so dramatic, though—mismatched from the start. And what does that mean for this potential kid, for any future he ever might have had caught between the two of us.

"But go back to the part where you're trying to say this is all your fault," says Dani, tugging me back to her intense gaze. "What do you even mean by that? Because none of this—" She spreads her hands out as though this whole tangle is hovering in the air in front of her, here in the safety of her tree fort.

"I know, all right?" Anger rises up inside me almost like her words are a stick that's stirred up a bucket of river water, mud that had settled once more spinning up to the surface. I feel clouded with feelings I haven't been able to feel since all of this started. "Everyone keeps telling me that none of this is my fault, blah blah blah, but if it's not my fault, whose is it?" There, okay? My fault for getting pregnant, my fault for not figuring out he was apparently sleeping with a legit crazy person. My fault for not making him understand how I actually felt about the whole getting-married idea (eject! eject!), and maybe even my fault for whatever happened on the snowmobile. "Everyone thinks I'm suicidal, Dani. Nobody even knows who Kendall really is. I probably can't get an abortion, and even if I can, I should probably use my money to pay for my teeth, since my mom lost her job and we have no insurance. But I can't..." Peace breathing. "I can't have a baby."

Dani doesn't try to talk, to be logical. She just squeezes me into a tight hug, then pushes me over and covers me up with her blankets. "I'm going to talk to Momma Fran," she says, climbing down from the tree. "You'll be staying here tonight."

THEN

(TO SCOTT, WITH COFFEE)

Do you believe that, what Dani said about us being mismatched? At any other point in our lives, the age wouldn't have made a difference, but it did for us. It really did. I don't know what else to say. I've been telling stories about your past, but I miss you here in the present.

Remember that one night when we walked all around campus in the dark, after your team lost so badly they had to run the clock at the end of the game? We didn't have a lot to say to each other, I suppose, other than endless choruses of "I miss you" and "I love you," and was that so terrible? Sometimes it bothered me when that happened, but other times those words felt like all we needed to stay close. I remember when you put your arms around my shoulders and pulled me close and we marveled at how our hip bones fit together "like a puzzle," you said, mine locking in right beneath yours. We walked with our bodies intertwined like that for several hours, keeping our balance as if by magic as long as we held closely together and moved in sync.

"When you get down here, we can get an apartment," you said, like you always said.

"We can get coffee in the mornings before heading to class," I said.

You laughed at me then, and said you would just enjoy the smell.

"That's a little creepy," I said, but when we stopped to make out on a shaded bench, I knew we were both thinking about that someday life, about our someday morning coffee.

NOW

I hold the cup close, but not too close, to Scott's nose. I stopped for the good stuff, no stupid hospital cafeteria coffee today, and I can't help feeling weird when I talk about kissing him even though nobody else is in the room right now.

"Wake up," I say, but I'm not sure I believe anymore that it's going to happen. "Open your eyes and smell this yummy caramel latte." This is totally silly, and I'm not sure how long I can keep it up. The guy in this bed is a stranger to me, a waxy face, clumsily shaven, his hair far too long to be my boyfriend. Scott never ever let his hair grow past the tips of his ears, and he frequently criticized Joey's shaggy mop and offered to "clean it up" for him. This makes me smile. "Hey, do you remember that time you chased Joey around the house with the clippers? Remember how he screamed?" Remember how you called him a little girl and how I stopped laughing and told you there was nothing wrong with being a girl, that the word girl wasn't an insult to throw around? Remember how you looked at me like you were going to argue but then realized you didn't have an argument?

A shadow moves, flickers over his face, and for the briefest instant my heart jumps—so many feelings clattering together inside me in that millisecond before I realize it's not Scott waking up but someone behind us entering the room, the reporter guy from before. The cute one.

"Hello," he says, and his voice is clear and particular—the kind of voice that's been trained for public speech. "You probably don't remember me."

"Tom." I remember the way I told him he couldn't use me in his news story or whatever. "You're the one who told Joey that Kendall's story doesn't match up, right?"

He shrugs, his shoulders reaching up toward his little sea-shell ears. Seriously, I can imagine him as a toddler, his family gathered around to pinch his adorable little cheeks, telling him his face needs to be on the television. "Yeah, that's me. Tom Baker from channel seven." He smiles an apology. "I left the camera by the door this time."

I look away, fixing the plastic lid back on my coffee since it doesn't seem like the aroma is going to lure my boyfriend out of his middle ground between sleep and waking.

"Taylor, right? You were his girlfriend."

"Yeah." I don't correct his verb tense because who am I fooling. My boyfriend is a couch cushion who now occasionally moves when his feet are poked with pins and who once cleared his throat or possibly mumbled his brother's name.

"You're the one who started the memory jar thing, right?"

"Well, my therapist started it, really." I think about Emily in the waiting room with her glue gun and all those little memory jars she's making, how nobody will say it but everyone is afraid that she's making them for her brother's funeral. I turn to look at Tom again, because really, how long can I pretend that this coffee lid is more interesting than his face? "So, tell me what else you found out about Kendall. If the whole sister thing is fake, what else is a lie?"

"Wait." Tom-the-beautiful-news-reporter pulls out the chair at the foot of Scott's bed and sinks into it like he's lost all ability to hold up his own spindly weight. "I'm sorry. From the start, you know, it's uncomfortable to come in here—*your boyfriend's had a traumatic brain injury, would you like to do an interview?*" He shakes his head. "And then I come back because my boss is like, Go back, Tom, you've got to get this story, and I talk to his sister and she's not saying much, so I'm trying to figure out if I have anything I can use, anything I can make a story out of, and, I mean, I'm looking through the tape I have of you and Scott that first day, and there's like a little bit I could use but I'm not using it because you made it clear you weren't comfortable with the whole thing, and suddenly there's this other girl sitting there in the family waiting room and she's all, 'Oh, are you here from the news? Let me tell you all about Scott,' and I mean, I had *no idea* about you being pregnant at that point, but this Kendall girl is telling me all about how heroic he was and how her sister has uterine cancer, and I thought . . . " He spreads his hands in front of him, helpless. "I don't even know *what* to do with this."

I sip my coffee. "Is any of her story true?"

"I haven't exactly been able to figure that out," he says, "but one thing is clear. Kendall has some pretty serious issues. I found out pretty quickly that what she was telling us wasn't actually the whole story. Just a standard background search online showed me that she has literally hundreds of profiles, identities, addresses. I couldn't help digging deeper. Once I started feeding her various email addresses into the search, it got even weirder. There's a whole strand of identities where she claims that she and Scott are a couple. She has posts about their life together, including a fair number of photos. I can't verify if they're real. In some of her profiles, she mentions they've moved in together. In other identities, he's a sperm donor for her pregnancy. She's been very active in forums about uterine cancer and also a bunch of motherhood communities, including some where she posts photos of her belly, or a belly, anyway, claiming that *she's* pregnant." Tom holds up his hands like he's surrendering. "I know. It's messed up."

"Oh my god. I can't ... I can't even form words." Pregnant, comatose, suicidal, none of it compares to that mess. "This isn't a feel-good story anymore, is it?" I take a sip of my coffee. "Plus, it's not over. Probably I'll die of a back-alley abortion, and he'll wake up perfectly fine and well-rested and ride off into the sunset with Kendall."

"I would never put this on the news," Tom says, and I believe him.

"It would make a better reality show, anyway," I observe. "A slow motion trainwreck."

"This is so awkward."

"Did they ever have an actual relationship?" I don't want to know, but I have to know.

Tom rubs his elbow. "I talked to Scott's roommate, Terence. He knew Kendall from hockey, and he said Scott was friends with her for a while, or at least they got together to study, saw each other at the rink. Terrence says Scott stopped hanging out with her pretty abruptly a while back, a couple of months ago at least. Scott used the phrase 'too intense,' and Terence also said that Scott was getting a lot of calls and texts, even a string of weird deliveries—flowers and candy and once even this gigantic stuffed teddy bear dressed like a goalie. They assumed she was behind it."

"I don't know what to think about any of this." I sit back down in the chair. I sip my coffee, but the queasiness hits me as soon as the first mouthful hits my tongue and I have to take a few deep breaths to steady myself. I am so *sick* of feeling sick. I set the cup down on Scott's bedside table and open one of the little dinner mints I brought for him to smell.

THEN

(TO TOM)

We went to a wedding once, a two-hour drive from Sterling Creek. A cousin of his—I can't remember her name, to be honest, and maybe it was a little weird that I went along, but this was early in our relationship and we were desperate for time together and horrified at the thought of a weekend apart. It was the first time I'd ever been somewhere with Scott and his whole family. It was the first time I'd ever experienced what it was like to be squished into the car with siblings and two parents and a whole lot of goofy shenanigans. Road trip traditions, fighting over the car stereo, sharing junk food. All new to me.

At the wedding itself, I was shy and awkward, and one of Scott's aunts or whatever came up to us in the church before the ceremony even started and was like, "Oh, and when are *you two* getting married?" and I could feel my face heat up so I knew I was blushing like crazy. Scott squeezed my hand and smiled at her, making some kind of smooth non-answer as he did, but she gave me a wink that said something in secret old-auntie code about girls and nice young men and marrying and probably having a bunch of little children. I've never been the kind of girl who had a princess wedding dream, you know? In fact, I can remember a time when Dani and I went to play at this other little girl's house when we were like eight or nine, and the other girl kept trying to get me to pretend to marry her little brother, who had sticky fingers and no front teeth. The girl had all these pretty dresses and plastic high heels and bouquets of flowers, and she got so mad at Dani and me for not playing that she had her mom call our moms to come and get us early. Anyway, I was sitting there at this wedding, Scott and I holding hands with his thumb tracing little circles on the top of mine, and suddenly I had all these tears in my eyes.

"I hadn't pegged you for the crying-at-weddings type," he said to me after, the two of us dawdling around the edges of the milling crowd, sneaking little moments of intimacy amid all his relatives. I twirled around so my yellow dress spun in a circle, warm June air on my bare legs, and I felt like I could do anything.

"It wasn't the wedding," I said, and I wanted to write a poem right then—get down on the ground and chalk it out on the sidewalk, maybe. I felt like the words were so close, but I couldn't say them out loud the way Scott and his brother and sister just fit together, laughing or fighting with each other in a way that was comfortable and nice, even when it got mean or rough. Scott and Joey were like puppies or lion cubs, maybe, rough and tumble, and Emily was this prissy little mother hen always pulling them apart and putting them in headlocks and tugging on their ears, all with the kind of big-sister smile I'd never experienced. "I wish I had a brother or a sister," I said, and maybe he kind of understood, but then he laughed.

"They're a pain in the ass," he said. "Do you know how many times I wished I was an only child growing up?"

There were a lot of people with siblings who felt compelled to tell me that fact when they found out I was an only. I guess they imagined my life was filled with peace and quiet, that nobody stole my toys or fought over the remote control or whatever, that these little privileges of solitude would make up for never having an ally, a confidant, even a scapegoat. Someone to share the burden of being the child, someone to make at least half of the mistakes. "Your family is amazing," I said, and I twirled again. "Even if your aunt made me blush."

"I'd marry you in a heartbeat," he said, and he pulled me in for a kiss—right there in front of everyone. A deep kiss, too, so I couldn't help pulling back and checking who was watching, but he took my chin and brought my face around to his again. "We can have a house full of kids, and you can watch them fight all day long. Then we'll see how lovely you think siblings are."

NOW

Tom sits on the footstool and listens, and I'm proud of him for not getting up for his camera to capture his feel-good moment. Scott sleeps, or drifts there a little bit above or below sleep, who can say. I pop one of the dinner mints into my mouth and talk around it. "They had a ton of these little mints on all the tables at the reception, mixed with peanuts. Scott couldn't pass a candy dish without taking a handful, but he hated nuts, so he kept giving them to me." I can't believe what I'm about to say. "All night long I was eating handfuls of them, and, well, I had an upset stomach on the ride home. I had terrible gas." I laugh, remembering how mortified I was at the time, trying to hold it in, hoping nobody would guess it was me. "It was so bad in the back of the van that Scott's sister Emily started using these little disinfecting hand wipes to mask the smell, but everyone was too nice to tease me about it."

"They all blamed it on me," says Joey, walking in. "And if I recall, you did not correct this assumption."

"See what I mean about scapegoats?" I say.

Tom laughs. "Only children have to blame the dog."

"Oh, my mother is too much of a neat freak to have *animals* cluttering up her home." I make big sad eyes at him and Joey. "It was a sterile, lonely childhood for me."

"With no one to blame when you farted," says Tom.

"Maybe you should fart right now," Joey adds. "Wouldn't it be hilarious if that's the smell that wakes up my brother?" He steps close and does this thing that's supposed to be, like, a joking punch to the shoulder or something, but halfway through it turns into a sort of putting-his-arm-around-me kind of thing? I can't quite tell, but he leaves it there, his hand on my shoulder, and the weight of it feels like a brick.

"Gross," I say. "It's not like I can fart on demand. I'm not a middle school boy."

Still smiling, Tom looks around and seems to realize the oddity of his even being here, so far from his camera and still kind of reeling from this weird conversation, from everything. "Well, anyway, uh … I'm still in touch with Terence, and I could forward you all the information I found, if you want." He gets awkwardly to his feet.

Joey looks up. "Keep me in the loop," he says. Tom promises to email us both.

"Fucking *Kendall*," I say. "I don't even want to talk about it anymore." I squeeze my eyes shut, and Joey tightens his hold on me, pulling me into both of his skinny arms so my face smashes into his canvas jacket. He smells nice, like muscles and loud music, and I know those aren't real smells but it's true anyway. I let him hold me, and he lets me pull myself back together.

"Kendall?" A voice, thick and hoarse.

His voice. "Scott!"

He's blinking, his eyes all scrunched up like it's way too bright, but they're open and all three of us jump up and push in close, and then Tom runs for a nurse or maybe his camera, and Joey crowds in so we're both hovering over Scott, saying his name, exclaiming and crying. "Scott, *oh my god*. You're awake!"

"I'm thirsty," he croaks, and his eyes meet mine. "Where is she?"

"I'm here," I say, and I wipe eyes, my nose, whatever, on my sleeve. I'm a mess, but I'm *here*, oh my god, he's awake. "Do you remember? Do you remember me?"

"Easy," says Joey, and he reaches for the little swab we've been dabbing Scott's mouth with to keep it from drying out too much. "Let's not overwhelm him." Scott's face is flushed pink and hot to the touch, and I feel panic creeping into the corners of my joy.

"Water," says Scott, and he frowns and turns away from the swab, making a face like an angry toddler. "*No.*" His eyes slide closed, and I all but pounce on his chest, my hands trying to pull him up out of the bed.

"Scott!" He's burning up, his heart fluttering away beneath my hands.

"Taylor!" Joey grabs my hands, grapples me again into some kind of a hug/restraint, and I'm fighting him even as my brain is telling me I'm acting out of control, but Scott can't go back to sleep, he can't go—

"Scott!" Joey tightens his arms around me and I'm sobbing and Scott's eyes are closed as though they never opened, and this can't be the way it happens.

"Did he say 'Kendall'?" My voice is too high-pitched to be me. "Did he ask for her? Oh my god, oh my god." I want to kill her. I want to kill him. I want to kill myself. Joey's arms relax but stay wrapped around me, his hand stroking my hair.

"It's okay," he whispers, right into my ear, and he helps me down into the chair. "It's okay. It means nothing."

The nurse is there, and two doctors and I guess Scott's parents come in too, but he's sleeping again. The voices are concerned, there's beeping machines, talk of fevers and IVs, and Joey pulls me down the hall and past the family waiting room and into the stairwell to the parking garage, the whole time with one arm still wrapped around me like maybe we're freezing to death or maybe one of us is drowning and working hard to drag the other one under, too.

"What's going to happen?" I say, when the heavy door swings shut and we're finally free of the beeping and the strange freeze-frame of hospital time. "What's happening now?" My voice echoes in the concrete stairwell and I mean everything and nothing, and I don't want an answer, and he pushes me to the wall and I kiss him and he kisses me back but it's not so much kissing as much as it is trying to breathe in and out through someone else's lungs, trying to feel through someone else's heart, and we hold on to each other for what feels like forever and we cling and we kiss and we cry.

"I don't know," he says at last. "I don't know."

THEN

(TO JOEY)

I was about to break up with him. I almost jumped off a cliff, so you know. I'm all messed up. But I didn't jump, and I called him, and he yelled at me about the baby like that was the only thing about me jumping off a cliff that was important, like I was nothing to him but an incubator.

I shouldn't have gone to the island. I should have told him right away when he got there. I waited by the window that evening for him to come over, and I rehearsed the words I was going to say. *Scott. Listen. This isn't about the baby. This isn't about what happened before. This is about being realistic, and realistically, this isn't working.* That was my speech. I know it's stupid, but so is asking your seventeen-year-old girlfriend to marry you, my god. Is that a rational thing to do? Is it better or worse than promising a baby to a girl with a personality disorder?

He used the island against me, the romance of it but also the isolation of it. I was always at his mercy out there, and it put the balance of power off kilter. I don't know that I realized it at the time, but it was true. I was trapped, and I should have chewed off my own leg, you know? Instead I took that stupid ring and held on to it and got onto the snowmobile.

It's horrible, Joey. I made one demand. And because he was a good guy, and because he felt bad about yelling at me earlier, and who knows, maybe because he felt bad about hiding Kendall from me, Scott let me be in control. *He let me drive.*

I remember the sound, and now I don't know how I could ever have forgotten it. It happened so fast. The whine of the engine grew louder and louder and it wasn't me. I lifted my hand and screamed, I wasn't pushing the throttle, and he tried to reach around me, but we were accelerating so fast, the sled skipping across the snow, bouncing and flying, and he swore in my ear and got his hand around at last and pounded his fist on a red button and the engine quit just as we crashed. A crunch. Silence. There was somewhat of a moon, and a dark blue-black sky. There was snow in my eyelashes and the sound of a crunch was stuck in my ears, even though it was silent, so silent, and soft, and I think I fell asleep.

I remember the crunch, and I'm sorry to say that because it was awful and I wish I could stop hearing it. I wish I could never think about it again, but it was loud, and it was unmistakable. The crunch of something breaking, and then silence, and sleep, and that's when the blood fits in. It must have been a dream, my bloody stomach and me dying, and Scott reaching out his hand. That never happened, but I ... I wish it had. I was about to break up with him, but I didn't want to kill him. I couldn't get myself to step off a cliff, but I suppose I might have wanted to die, after all.

There was blood in real life, too. There were voices and bright lights shining at me. A man yelling, the stars spinning overhead, and things were confusing for a long time. I kept reaching for him, reaching for the red button, but there was nothing to stop and no one could hear me screaming. More engine whine and a mask over my face and I was about to break up with him but I was wearing his ring.

If I had done it, if I had pulled him aside and said, *Scott. Listen. This isn't about the baby.* If I had refused to let him lure me out the door and onto that stupid snowmobile. *This is about being realistic, and realistically, this isn't working.* It wasn't the worst break-up line in the world. And if I had done it, none of this would have happened. That moment on the snowmobile wouldn't have happened, and that crunch. That crunch should never have happened.

That crunch is my fault.

NOW

"This is so messed up," Joey says for about the fiftieth time. We're sitting in his car, which is running but not moving. My mouth still tastes like his, and my hands are sweating.

This is insane. I fight the queasiness, the pieces of my new memory that are trying to suffocate me. "It was all my fault." I mean the kiss; I mean the crash. I mean the world.

"I don't know what I was thinking." He's said that about twenty times. "He didn't look so good, you know." Eighteen times. "I don't blame you, Taylor." Fifty. "What else do you remember?" Ten.

"Why would he say *her* name?" I say, and I've lost count on that one.

Joey puts the car in gear, finally, and eases out of the parking spot.

"Where are we going?"

He doesn't answer, but I don't really care, so I sit back and look out the window. It's cold today, and icy, and I can't stop thinking about the crash, the whine, the crunch. I liked it better when I couldn't remember, maybe. My phone buzzes, and I'm scared to look. I haven't gotten any more pictures of chopped-up babies, but that doesn't keep me from cringing every time a text pops up.

It's Dani. *Got a lead on some possibilities for that other thing,* she says. If my mom saw that, she'd think I was doing drugs for sure. I probably should be. I bet Celeste could hook me up. Whine and crunch. And fucking Kendall.

"Do you really think of yourself that way?" he says.

"What?" What way? I stare at Dani's text and wonder if I can go through with it, with that other thing. How weird would it be to walk into a clinic and walk back out with a do-over, a second chance. I feel claustrophobic in this car, in this family. I have the urge to open the door and jump out, to roll through the snowy ditch like I'm in an action flick, jump to my feet and run. Joey drives too fast.

"Do you think you're messed up, like you're broken or something? Did you really try to kill yourself?" He looks at me too long, too intensely, for someone who's supposed to be driving.

Roll, jump, run. I would kill myself, obviously, jumping from a moving vehicle. I watch the trees flashing past, skeletons standing sentinel. "I don't know what to do."

"It's not your fault," he says. "I know I blamed you at first for what happened to my brother. But right now I'm worried about *you*."

My phone buzzes again. *Wisconsin will do it with any adult relative over 25. Could find someone to pretend. Have to drive to Madison probably. Or could try to get court bypass. Good time to call?*

I stare at the message. Is it that simple, then? Grab an older friend, say she's my sister, drive down to Madison or whatever, sign it away. Slight cramping, a little spotting, everything disappears. I've done enough searching around the Internet to have a pretty good idea what I'd be getting myself into, even this court bypass business. The screen goes dark and Dani's message is gone. I'm alone in a car with a huge mistake. Well, two of them, really. "He's awake," I say, and I touch the screen, bring Dani's text up again. "I can't believe he's awake."

Can't talk now, I text back. *Busy having a look at my life, my choices.* It's a joke that isn't. She'll get it.

"Did Tom tell you about Kendall faking her own death?" says Joey. He turns left at the mall, away from the center of town, and I know he's heading toward Grave Lake. What would it take for us to get back out to the island? The snowmobile is gone, but the ice is solid enough for the car by now. The daylight is fading, leaving the sky looking like a washcloth that has seen too many spin cycles, too many mascara stains. "So yeah, the deeper Tom looked into the situation, the weirder it got," Joey goes on. "One of Kendall's Internet identities, or whatever you call them, 'died' of uterine cancer. Maybe it was supposed to be her fake sister, I don't know. She made all these cancer friends and then she died and they all donated to a children's cancer charity in her fake name. All of this while posting as other identities, even in the same forum. What the fuck, right?"

"I'm the one who kissed *you*," I say. We're definitely on the way to Grave Lake now, the long straight stretch through the swamp, desolate and empty. Something in my chest tries to claw its way out via my desperately pounding heart, and I think I could make him turn back if I were to speak up, but an equally powerful desire to see the place again, to remember the ending and put to rest the questions, keeps me silent.

He ignores me. "Can you believe that? Do you think we need a restraining order?"

I'm stuck on the sound of him saying her name, still trapped in the moment he looked into my eyes and asked where she was. Kendall. *Adoption. I could live with that.* That was one of the slogans from my mystery pro-life texter. As if being alive is the only variable that matters—life at any cost, any quality. "I mean, if we get the cops involved … " I can get a court bypass. I can pretend she doesn't exist. "I did try to kill myself," I say. "But I don't think I'm suicidal enough to succeed. I'm just sort of stuck and don't know what to do, and that seemed like a way to make the decisions not matter anymore."

He slows the car, turns into the road for the public access. "You know, people have kids all the time when they're young, and it's not really the end of the world." He eases the car down the boat ramp and out onto the lake. "I think we can get pretty close to the island. There's a sort of a road plowed out to the fish houses in the next bay, but we'll have to walk from there. I have an extra hat and a scarf in the back."

My phone buzzes. *Your life, your choices, are beautiful. CHIN UP!!!!*

I barely have time to smile before it buzzes again, but this time it's not Dani. *We NEED 2 talk abt the poss of adoption? PLS!* Followed by another one: *Abortion is MURDER and u will be a MURDERER.* The car bounces across the snowy road, tires spinning here and there on the windswept ice. I hang on to the edge of the seat and dial the last number. Far away, it rings, a hollow sound, until it stops. No message.

In the dim beams of the headlights I can see the square shapes of three or four fish houses clumped together up ahead. Joey drives more carefully now, leaning forward to see where the makeshift road leads. "I'm going to have to park it here, I think," he says, but *park* is too intentional a word for what happens when the car sort of slides to a stop and the front tires sink into what I hope is deep snow and not a gaping hole in the ice. "Damn it." He puts the car into reverse and tries to back onto firmer ground, but the tires whine in a way that any Minnesotan can easily recognize as the sound of "Oh shit, we're stuck."

I pull on my gloves and stick my phone into the zipper pocket on my jacket. At least I'm wearing boots, even though they're not great boots, and my toes are already a tiny bit cold. My jacket has a hood, but it's flimsy.

"It's okay," Joey says. "Let me take a look at the front end, see if I can get us unstuck." He points away from the fish houses. "The island is right over there, I'm pretty sure. If we're lucky, the snow will have a good crust, and we can walk right on top."

I sit in the car for a few minutes, watching Joey poke around in the front. After a while he gets back in, leaving the driver's door ajar. He shifts into reverse and tries to ease the car backward but stops as soon as the tires spin again. "We sank through a layer of half-frozen slush," he says. "Nasty stuff, but the ice is good underneath. A layer of water on top, so that shit is slippery. Can you drive while I try to push?"

I get out and walk around to the driver's side, but Joey wants to show me the slush, and the tires sitting on glare ice. "You don't want to go hard on the gas," he says, "or we'll spin out more of this slush and then we'll never get out. Just go easy."

I shake my head. "I don't know, Joey. What if I accidentally make it worse?" My phone rumbles inside my zipper pocket, and I have another text from the same number.

PLS taylor don't make any decision til i see u we would love the baby like our own! CHOOSE LIFE!!!

"It's Kendall," I say, and I hold up the phone so Joey can see. "It's been her all along." Somehow he's become my ally in this even if he doesn't realize it. "Look at this one, Joey, oh my god. She's texting me more *pictures of chopped-up fetuses*, trying to scare me out of having an abortion. That girl is horrifying. She needs help."

"Abortion?" says Joey, and he takes my phone to look. "Oh god, what is this. Wait. Are you planning...?" He's trying to hide his distress. "*Our* baby?"

I hold up my hand. Whoa, whoa. "What?" I take my phone back, take a step away. I shouldn't have kissed him. This is getting too weird. "I have a right to make this choice." The wind slaps at my face and my exposed ears.

Joey zips up his stupid little coat. "I didn't mean it like *our* baby," he says. The wind tries to drown out his voice, but he talks louder. "But Scott's waking up and we'll find out what's going on and I just meant ... well, I told you I'd take care of you. Of you both." He stuffs his hands into his jacket pockets, and I pull my arms around myself and try to keep all my rage from spinning out of control. "My brother may or may not get better," he continues, "but I'm here. This baby ... do you get it? This baby could be the best thing we have left out of all of this, and you—you're our family, too, Taylor. I want you to understand I'm not a stupid kid, not Scott's reckless little brother, the one who had to go to rehab. I can be better for you."

I'm shaking my head, but it's so windy—my hair snaps into my eyes, and I can't believe this. "Joey, it doesn't ... it doesn't work like that."

"Why not, though?"

He moves toward me, and I step back again. I feel all this adrenaline, this fight-or-flight feeling. I'm not scared of Joey, but I'm sort of uncomfortable with this level of intensity, you know? I remember Joey's rehab, but it wasn't for drugs—it was like Joey was doing self-destructive things, thrill-seeking or something. I keep backing up, my boots crunching in the snow off the edge of the plowed path.

Joey holds up both hands, palms out. "It's okay. I'm sorry. I'm in love with you. I know that doesn't make sense, not now. You're my brother's girlfriend. His *fiancée*. But I can handle it. Like I said, I'm sorry I kissed you. It wasn't the right thing to do. It wasn't the right time." He shakes his head, gestures to the car. "Will you please drive while I push, and I'll take you back to the hospital or home or wherever you want to go, and we can talk about it or not, but I just want you to understand that I'm not going anywhere, whatever happens with Scott. I'm here for you, and I'm here for his baby."

I turn away. "I can't, not yet." I can't look at him because I'm so embarrassed and so taken aback and so flattered and so unnerved by the way my heart feels when I look in his direction. It's too cold to stand here, and it's too weird to get in the car with him, so I start walking in the direction I think is toward the island. It's not that far. Maybe I can start a fire, like Scott taught me. I remember the thrill of that little structure igniting, and there's at least a part of me that thinks a fire like that could be a sort of magic, you know? To pull Scott back to us, and maybe to push back my guilt, too.

I kissed Joey, but it was just a weird thing that can happen. There are stages to grief, and obviously one of them is completely messed up. I'm sure Celeste could explain it. I keep moving, and it feels good to walk. My legs warm up with the exertion, and the wind is at my back, holding my hood against the back of my head. It's not that cold. I want to see the island. I want to remember.

"Taylor, wait! Let me get you a hat!" I hear his voice, but I don't slow down. I'm fine. Everything's fine, and I don't need Joey to be here for me.

THEN

He yelled at me when I called him, fury in his voice. His first response was this flash of anger, and here I was calling him for help, for understanding. *I had no right to hurt myself, I had no right to hurt the baby.* Well, that was bullshit. It was my body, not his, and my life. If I wanted to throw myself into a frozen mine pit, baby and all, that was my decision, and he could at least act like he cared about *me* at least as much as he cared about some sort of *idea* inside me.

"You're just as selfish as my stupid brother," he said, and I decided to break up with him. Now I remember Joey and the time he spent in rehab that time, and I feel bad for not giving Scott a chance to really explain what he meant by that. I wasn't interested, at the time, but maybe I *was* really being selfish. Maybe it wasn't anger in his voice but fear.

Joey had a dirt bike and he did something dumb in a gravel pit, "acted like he had a death wish as usual," according to Scott. I remember the bitterness in Scott's voice when he told me, the way his hands squeezed into fists. He worried about his little brother's recklessness, and the whole family started to think that there was something more to it than being an adrenaline addict. Maybe, like Scott claimed, Joey *wanted* to die. When he flipped his bike on top of himself while climbing an impossibly steep hill, when he was held together mostly by scars and stitches, his family had had enough, and they decided he needed more help than they could give him. I was pretty new to their family dynamic during this time, and Joey was just this kid a grade younger than me who was kind of a little bit dangerous. At school, people said he was nuts, but in a way that meant they were impressed by his craziness. They told stories of his epic cliff-dives or jumping open water on his snowmobile and shook their heads. "That kid's straight up loco," I remember one boy saying when the rumors started going around school that Joey was out for six weeks at the treatment center down in Duluth. "Those shrinks are set up to help girls who cut themselves, not crazy assholes like him." I remember being a little bit scared of this loose cannon in my new boyfriend's family.

Joey came back from the program with a therapist and a kind of dark, experienced quality that made the girls crowd in close, hoping to save him. He no longer scared his family with his apparent death wish. He was quiet and slouchy, and he looked like he needed to curl around a guitar or a skateboard.

His hair hung in his eyes. His dirtbike was locked in the shed, and his snowmobile was destined for someone else's destruction.

NOW

Every step toward the island is a step away from smoothing things over with Joey and going back to the hospital to sit at the side of my brain-injured boyfriend whose first word upon waking up was another girl's name. A step away from getting warm, too, though I still have this idea of making a fire, of kindling my memory of that final night, of finding some clue that will absolve me, maybe.

My feet crunch along the top of the snow, which glows softly in the gathering dark. I'm thinking about my memory, how strangely the images slide into place until I'm pretty sure I caused the crash even if I can't finish out the memory entirely. What if I did it on purpose? What if I was really trying to kill us both? The details fall into empty holes between images like shadows settling into all the hollow places, chasing out the imagined shapes my brain has created to see through the darkness. What if *Kendall* did it? Could she have messed with the snowmobile in some way, thinking—what? What *is* she thinking? I can't even begin to guess. Was Scott rejecting her by marrying me instead of giving her imaginary sister our baby? Did she try to kill us both in a jealous rage? What if, back at the hospital right now, Scott has woken up again and is telling everyone the whole story, about Kendall and everything? What if he doesn't wake up again at all? The uncertainty of all of it sits in my gut like a stone, the possibility that doubt will always be there—unanswered questions. I think of his feverish cheek, his bright eyes. Her name in his mouth.

I've been walking for six or eight years now, at least, but I'm still trying to ignore the chill seeping in through the soles of my stupid boots. My cheeks and the tip of my nose sting from the wind gusting around the edges of my hood, and my thighs feel like heavy planks crawling with biting ants. There's no sign of the island, not even a dark shadow on the horizon. Nothing around but the endless eerie glow—I feel like I'm walking on the moon, except with every step my feet weigh twice as much. I can't get lost walking on a lake, right? I mean, it's a big open space, surrounded on all sides by the shoreline, with a giant island in the middle. Even in the dark, I'm not going to walk past an entire island. Even so, the anxiety sits in my belly, and its presence does not help to warm me.

Inside my jacket pocket, my phone rumbles, and I stop to fish it out, but the zipper takes me too long with my gloves on, and I miss the call. I slip one glove off to check, and it's from that number, the please-consider-adoption number. Fucking

Kendall. The voicemail message icon pops up with a soft beep, and I'm clicking through menus, trying to access the message, my fingers freezing, when the screen flashes and the phone buzzes again. Text from Dani. I back out of voicemail and pull up her message, shifting my weight from one frozen foot to the other. My hair, whipping in the wind, escapes from my hood and obscures my vision. I drag it back out of my face with my still-gloved hand, trying to twist it at the back of my neck, but my hood falls down and an icy blast shoots down the back of my neck. It's seriously too cold. I need to get to that fire or turn back and let Joey win this round. Whatever, I need to keep moving. I turn around to let the wind push my hair back off my face.

Got you a pretend aunt, looks 25, trustworthy. Will make appt right now online, but only if it's what you want. LOVE YOU.

My feet are so cold. I hop up and down, still trying to twist my hair back, but my glove is too full of static and I pull it off with my teeth and walk backward for a few steps, trying to wrestle everything into place. I have no clue what direction I'm supposed to be heading anymore, and my eyes are blinded by the light of my phone anyway. Whatever, it's not snowing. I can always follow my own footprints back, and why hasn't Joey run after me, anyway? After that speech about how he'll always be there for me.

For me and the baby. Whatever. What is it that makes everyone in the world feel like the instant two cells stick together inside my uterus, they all should have more say in what happens inside my body than I should? I think I could save about a million more lives than this one potential life if I can move forward and become a cardiologist, but I can't have a baby. Not now. I keep walking, my glove still hanging in my teeth, and focus my attention back on Dani's message.

It's what I want. My thumbs pause, poised above the bright screen, my feet crunching below me in the darkness, headed in no particular direction. I hit send.

It happens so fast, so stupid. Crunch. I'm walking alone in a monotony of footsteps, my best friend's capslocked love and this broken choice sent from my frozen fingers, and, too sudden and stupid, my foot breaks through, sinks through slush and slides on wet ice beneath—in a heartbeat I'm pitching forward; my phone skitters off across the ice and my hands punch twin holes through the slush in front of me. Cold seeping into me, frigid, stunned, I scramble for anything to push against, but there's nothing but ice cold water and panic—I'm sure I've gone through the ice and I feel my heart stutter, slow, until somewhere deep beneath I find solid ice and push, my knee sinking, push up to standing, and the wind hits me full and frozen.

The cold is so intense that my brain almost immediately dismisses the pain, leaving me with both arms soaked to the armpits in water a half degree from being frozen solid—they hang, numb and useless. My left knee is wet through, my jeans freezing to my skin, and my right boot is filling with water. I don't know. I'm shivering in a way that alarms some distant part of me, a part that isn't trying to figure out if I'm standing up or if I'm alive. I can't feel my foot, but I don't fall over so I take a step. I can hear water sloshing over my toes and that distant part tells me I need to empty my boot,

I need to get dry, I need to maybe take off the wet clothes or something, but I'm not sure where my hands are except that they're wrapped in a wave of pain that I can't feel so much as I hear it—the sound of a waterfall pushing me underwater, a surround-sound television stuck on static, my teeth clattering against each other inside my head.

Walk. I have to get warm. I have to move. I spend too long searching for my phone, and when I find it (shattered screen but not too wet), I can't seem to close my fingers around it much less press the buttons to call for help. Where the fuck is Joey? He should be here with that stupid extra hat. The wind is in my face and I need to follow my footprints back, no magic fire, just fast walking and violent shivering and I think it's good to shiver but I can't remember why, and I lift my arm to catch my balance and the cold air pushes itself through my wet jacket and I can feel my heart slow like a down-shifting engine, and it's scary. I bring my arms in tight again and think of the baby I'm scheduling out of me and thinking about how they'll find my body and there will be no more privacy, pregnant teen found frozen on Grave Lake. I pull everything in tighter around the middle of me. I lean into the wind and will my legs to hold me even if I can't feel them.

I can do this. I'm not going to freeze to death on this awful lake, and I'm not going to be one of those people Scott told me about who goes hypothermic and takes off all their clothes, though at this point I'm not sure I would be able to take my clothes off even if I wanted to. There's a test for it, I remember now, or at least I remember Scott showing me something, but when I try to recall exactly what it was my brain goes all foggy and I find myself standing still, staring at my hands. Why am I not wearing gloves? I don't know where they are. Did I drop them? My hands look funny. I reach down for a shadow on the ground, but my hands close on nothing and I'm crawling and I don't think this is the way to the island. *Focus.* There's a baby here. I have to save it.

A phone ringing. It's in my hand but I can't bring it up to my ear.

Taylor? TAY?

Mom? I don't know if I'm speaking or thinking. I'm so tired. I bring my head down to the phone since I can't move my arm. I can't move anything.

Taylor, don't do anything stupid!

I smile. "Too late," I say, but the phone slides away from me, and I'm not sure she hears.

THEN

My mother. She took me to the ocean, once, in California, when I was too little to understand we were there to say good-bye to her mother, who was dying of cancer. "This is where your mama grew up," she said, and I remember the way she held my hand, the way she walked with bare feet over the sand. Her steps were lighter than they usually were, even though her face was sad.

"Why did we move to Minnesota?" I drew in the white, soft sand with my finger. I wrote my name in giant, lopsided letters.

"You were born there, sweetheart," she said. She sat in the sand beside me and traced her finger over the heart I had drawn, traced the letters, MOM. "It's your home."

NOW

I'm staring at the snow, dragging my hand through the crusty top layer. Mom. I don't see the phone. I can still hear her voice, saying my name, and I want to curl up tight into this darkness but I have to get up, get moving.

I'm not cold anymore. I still can't find my feet or my legs and everything slows down when I uncurl and I wonder if it's worth it, but there's something urgent tugging at my belly and I see the word MOM in the snow or the sand and I want to live. I push on, stumbling.

"Taylor? Holy shit!" Arms pulling me in, hands running up and down me. "Oh god, you're soaked."

I try to tell him but the words won't line up. My mouth belongs to someone else.

"Get in the car," he says, but he's already half-carrying me, half-dragging me, and I fall against the seat. I can't stop shivering. "I couldn't figure out who to call." He's pulling at something, and I realize it hurts, which is a new sensation.

"Stop—" My voice doesn't sound right. Is my actual tongue frozen? My boots. He's pulling off my boots.

"Sorry. This heater sucks, but I'm going to have to—" He's tugging at something else and I try to pull away. He's unbuttoning my jeans. "Sorry, Tay. No time for modesty when you're this cold."

He pulls off the rest of my wet things and wraps me in a blanket and his own jacket. I can feel the pressure of his hands and as my body starts to thaw out it only feels colder, but mostly I am nauseous and sleepy and Joey pulls a hat down over my head and presses my hands between his own, then pulls up his shirt and puts my hands against his chest. The heater rattles on full blast but I can't feel any actual heat.

"I called Celeste at the hospital," he says. "I told her you took off in the cold, and she said she's sending help." *Celeste.* I can't quite place who she is, but she sounds like an angel. Joey's eyes are worried but I don't remember why.

"I was scared if I went after you, you'd run away even more. I had to peel part of the wall off one of those fish houses to put under the wheels, but I got the car unstuck," he says, indicating out the window with his chin and then pressing his fingertips to my neck. "Your pulse seems slow."

I swear I'm getting colder every second now, shivering harder—my lungs fill with air for the sole purpose of maintaining some kind of low growling wail that I can't stop, can't control. Joey flicks the switch on the heater a couple of times, fiddles with the vents, folds his lanky body around me in an awkward pile in the passenger seat. "Are you going to make it, Tay? I'm going to start toward shore, try and meet them."

"Hungry," I say, which is a weird thing to say, but my mouth at least forms a word. "Everything hurts." The shivering settles, pins and needles in my feet. Who is them? I try to move my hand, but it barely floats up. I think about opening the door, falling to the ground. The snow seems softer.

"Taylor." He kisses me, I'm pretty sure, even though everything feels a step or two from real and I can't remember if I should kiss him back or not. Anyway, I close my eyes and I think I stay alive.

THEN

(JOEY)

The sheriff met us at the boat landing, and the first responders were there within a minute. You were warming up by then, even asking him questions about the accident investigation, but they put you in the ambulance and ran some warm fluids through your IV. I rode with you and made sure you stayed awake, even though nothing you said made sense. Like that stuff about your mom talking to you on the phone, which didn't happen. Your mom hasn't left your side since you got to the hospital, but you didn't even have your phone anymore by the time you got to me.

Scott hasn't been awake since we saw him. Since we heard him speak. I know, I *know*. Don't worry about that. My mom printed out all of Tom's research and got a restraining order on

Kendall, but then Terence called us to say that the police found some weird software on Scott's phone and computer, like parents might use to spy on their kids. There was also a stuffed animal that had a recording device in it? Some kind of wireless nanny-cam thing. Creepy as hell, but somehow it's starting to make sense to me. Scott always thought he could fix everyone else's problems without getting hurt by them himself.

It's not good, Tay. His temperature spiked up super high, an infection in his brain or around it. I guess it's pretty common with a skull fracture. My mom said they knew he was sick, that they've been watching him closely for a few days now. They're giving him hardcore antibiotics, but it's not working. When he woke up, do you remember how his face was kind of flushed? Right after we left the hospital, he had some kind of seizure, and it wouldn't stop. They've had to put him on some pretty strong medications, just to keep the seizures down.

Anyway, it's been a rough night, and I'm just glad you're okay. You scared me, Tay. I didn't mean to overstep, but I want you to know that a lot of people love you. I mean that, as a brother. As a friend. And I want you to know that's something that stays the same no matter what happens to Scott or what you decide. You've got me on your side.

NOW AND THEN

(COLLISION)

There are moments that are missing and moments I'm not sure I remember right. The sheriff, for one, what he said right before they put me in the ambulance.

"You get yourself together, young lady," he said, or at least that's how I heard it. "No sense letting one freak accident set the course of your life."

"Accident?"

"You and that Janson kid. We just closed the investigation. Cause of the crash was a stuck throttle, happens sometimes when it's icy and damp. You couldn't have stopped it without turning off the engine." He cleared his throat, and the whole sky full of stars spun behind his head while he waited to say more. The stuck throttle? So it wasn't my fault. *It isn't my fault.*

"You kids think you're invincible, that you have this grand life stretching out ahead of you like an empty page. A book you'll fill in later, when you have time to slow down. Your life is *now*, kid. Your life is here, and it can change on a dime."

NOW

My mom won't let go of my hand. "He's not doing well," she says, and I know she's talking about Scott. "We can't lose you both."

I'm not lost. I'm warm and alive, probably still pregnant, and my mom is holding my hand. "I thought it was my fault," I say. My voice is shaky and new. "He gave me a ring, but I can't get married. I can't have a baby."

She squeezes my hand. "I was looking for a stamp. I opened the junk drawer in the kitchen, and I saw how you'd ripped up those awful pictures. I knew, then. It all fell into place."

"I'm scared."

She sniffles, and her other hand comes up over her face. "Listen. I know I'm not perfect. I know I would be a better mom all around if I'd had you like six or eight years later, when I'd figured out some things about being a person. But it's not the end of the world, and this is not the end of your life, by any means."

I take a slow breath and turn my attention to the ceiling tiles. "Dani made me an appointment," I say. I've made my decision about Madison and my pretend aunt, but somehow it's important to know what my mother says about this, whether she can still love me if I chose myself over my potential kid. "I couldn't figure out how to tell you."

She takes a long time to respond, but she doesn't stop holding my hand. Finally she takes a breath and whispers, "I love you, Taylor, and I understand why you didn't want to tell me. I'm not sure I would have told me either. But I won't let you go to Wisconsin with Dani and a person pretending to be your family."

She always does this to me. I pull my hand away, and I want to roll over and face the wall until she leaves. I want to get an abortion to spite her, to prove that I'm not always going to be under her thumb. That's stupid. I glare at the ceiling, but the anger rises.

"I mean, I'll go with you. Taylor. *I'll be there*," she says, and she puts her hand on my shoulder. "God, honey, if you only knew how much being a grown-up is made up of screwing up, and how hard it is to admit this to your headstrong daughter who already thinks of your life as a flat line, static and set."

She reaches for my chin, pulls my face around to hers, and I see in her eyes how much she means this. "This thing with my job, the office closing, everything falling apart—it may seem like a terrible thing, but it opens up some options. It's not going to be easy, but we can rethink a path that will let you have this baby, if that's what you want. I'm here for you."

It's everyone's favorite thing to say. They're all here for me. I look at my mother's face—a face I've grown used to studying, looking for cues—but there's nothing there but love. I think about Scott's mom, sitting vigil by her son's bed, watching him slip away.

I think about all the things we leave unsaid, all the ways we make ourselves unknowable even to the ones we love. "I'm going to be a doctor," I say. "A cardiologist *and* a poet. I'm going to work my ass off to get scholarships, and I'm sorry for not telling you sooner." I look away so I'm not tempted to read too much into my mom's response, but I can't believe how happy it makes me to have finally told her.

My IV bag is empty, and a nurse with a stern face nods crisply at my mother and goes about taking out the needle and taping my hand up with a cotton ball. She's all business, silent and efficient, and she doesn't even warn me that she's activating the automatic blood pressure cuff, which feels like it will slice my arm in two. She frowns, taps a few numbers into the computer and turns to go.

"Excuse me," Mom says. "Now that she's not connected to the IV pole, can Taylor leave the room for a bit? She needs to see her boyfriend."

"Doctor Forrest wants to try a Doppler," the nurse says, without looking at me.

"What's that?" I want to make her speak to me, but she continues to address my mother.

"Check for fetal heartbeat," she says. "May or may not

work at this stage, but he wants a listen. He'll do an ultra-sound if we can't get something from the outside."

"Wait." I need her to look at me. "Are you saying we're going to hear a heartbeat?"

"Hear it or see it, if it's there." She nods. "What your body has been through tonight—plenty of folks don't ever see the other side of a hypothermic event like this." She finally makes eye contact. Her eyes, I'm surprised to see, are welled and shiny. "You're very lucky."

Celeste is at the door, her face serene. "I wanted to check if there was anything you need," she says, and her eyes slide briefly in my mom's direction. She says a lot of things without speaking, and I remember how I told her she was good at empathy. Is there anything I need? Is there?

"They're checking for a heartbeat," I say. "Can you ... can you make it so I don't have to hear it?" My mother squeezes my hand.

THEN AND NOW

Nobody blames me. We murmur farewells like a lullaby chorus, singing him down somewhere deeper than sleep. Into our stories—our past and our future.

"I'm keeping the appointment," I say, over the body of his brother draped in plastic tubing and medical tape. Joey's eyes slide shut, but not fast enough. I reach for him, for those narrow shoulders in need of a hug. "Hey," I say, and I run my thumbs across the tears on his face. "Joey. It's intense right now, but we'll heal."

I can't explain the relief that comes with remembering, the way it feels when the gaps are filled—even if there are things I can never know, no matter how much I want it. I want to believe it was Kendall who twisted everything, and I'm glad that thanks to all of this, her family is working with social workers and such to get her the help she needs. But there's something to what Joey said, too, about Scott wanting to fix people. I wonder what he was fixing about me.

I can't forget him saying her name when he woke. I can't forget him yelling at me on the phone, and the crunch in the snow.

"This is not a story like that," I say, and I take the hand in mine—the hand that no longer feels like a couch cushion but something less than that, even. "It's not about a girl and her sad ending, or about a boy and his sad ending either. It has some good parts—the parts we told to call the boy back—and it has some secret parts that remain unwritten. This story is not about an ending at all, even though it has endings inside it." I look up at Joey, and what we share is complicated. I'm not sure what the future holds, but I'm glad Joey didn't die in a dirt bike stunt, and I'm glad I stepped away from the edge of the mine pit, too. "This is a story that keeps moving forward."

Joey doesn't reach for me, but his presence there feels more solid, less like a pillar and more like an arch that's helping me hold this. We both look at Scott, whose chest no longer rises and falls beneath the sheet. The two of us can share our loss and our hope. I'm glad to know the crash wasn't entirely my fault, but blame no longer feels like the most important thread binding me to this tragedy. I hold the memory jar in my lap. It feels lighter now than it has for days, without all those words which this afternoon I shredded into a fine confetti. Joey watches as I twist open the top and pull out a small cellophane packet. My vision swims. I slip the ring on Scott's little finger.

"I loved you," I say, releasing his hand. "I'm sorry I was about to break up with you."

Joey shrugs into his jacket, no more secrets between us. His hands settle on my wheelchair, and together we leave this room behind us for good.

NOW

We keep moving forward. My hand reaches into the jar, churning through the fragile casings of our memories, and I imagine how wonderful it will feel, flinging these words away from me in a strong wind, a bloom of black and purple penmanship, spreading like a bruise and then healing all in a breath.

The doors to the brain injury ward slide open ahead of us, and Joey pauses beside the bank of elevators. The air seems to hum with questions, and I know there's more than one kind of moment that changes everything. "Where are we headed?" I say.

"You choose," he says, "but you don't have to make the decision alone." He pulls my chair carefully into a descending elevator—backward, so that when the doors slide open to the world outside, I will be ready to face anything.

About the Author

Elissa Janine Hoole has lived most of her life in northern Minnesota but has never driven a snowmobile. She prefers to cross frozen lakes on skis, especially if the outdoor adventure is followed by a steaming mug of coffee and a well-built fire. Elissa also teaches middle school writing and started this book with a purple pen on a magic note card during her creative writing club. She is the author of the YA novels *Sometimes Never, Sometimes Always* and *Kiss the Morning Star*. You can visit her online at ElissaJHoole.com.